Let's Enjoy Masterpieces!

Romeo and Juliet
羅密歐與茱麗葉

Original Author William Shakespeare
Adaptor Dan C. Harmon
Illustrator Nika Tchaikovskaya

WORDS
1000

MP3

Introduction

威廉・莎士比亞

William Shakespeare (1564~1616)

The world-famous playwright **William Shakespeare** was born of a middle class family in England. Since his family was rich, his childhood was very comfortable. However, he could not attend a university because his family lost its wealth when he was thirteen years old.

At the age of eighteen he married Anne Hathaway, who was eight years older than him, and later had three children with her. It is believed that Shakespeare began to write as a playwright around 1590. In the beginning of his writing career, he was just practicing and copying ideas from other authors. However, he worked hard and kept getting more and more popular. Finally, he achieved some success as an actor and a playwright and in 1594 became a leading member of the King's official playwright company, where he continued to write until his death.

He wrote thirty-seven plays, and his writings are generally divided up into four periods: historic plays, "joyous" comedies, tragedies, and tragic romantic comedies. His four well-known great tragedies include: *Hamlet*, *Othello*, *King Lear*, and *Macbeth*. They were written during the Period of Tragedies. The sonnets in his plays established his reputation as the best poet and the greatest dramatist the world has ever known.

He died on his fifty-second birthday on April 23, 1616 in Stratford-Upon-Avon, which was his birthplace. The people there still annually celebrate his death.

Romeo and Juliet

The setting is the beautiful city of Verona in Italy. There has been a long-running feud between the two main families: the Montagues and the Capulets.

One day, Romeo, the only son of the Montagues, sneaks into a ball being held by the Capulets. There, he meets Juliet, the daughter of the Capulets. They fall in love at first sight. Although they know their families are enemies, they cannot help but love each other. The next day they go to a monastery and get secretly married.

Meanwhile, Juliet's cousin Tybalt is furious that Romeo was present at the ball. He challenges Romeo to a duel. While traveling after the wedding, Romeo is confronted by Tybalt. Now considering Tybalt his kinsman, Romeo refuses to fight. However, Tybalt fatally wounded Mercutio, a friend of Romeo. Grief-stricken, Romeo manages to kill Tybalt.

Romeo and Juliet was a drama covering 5 acts and 24 scenes and was written in the middle of 1590. The magnificent poetic lines in the drama and the fate of two young lovers victimized by the feuds combine to make *Romeo and Juliet* one of Shakespeare's finest works as well as one of his most frequently performed plays.

How to Use This Book

本書使用說明

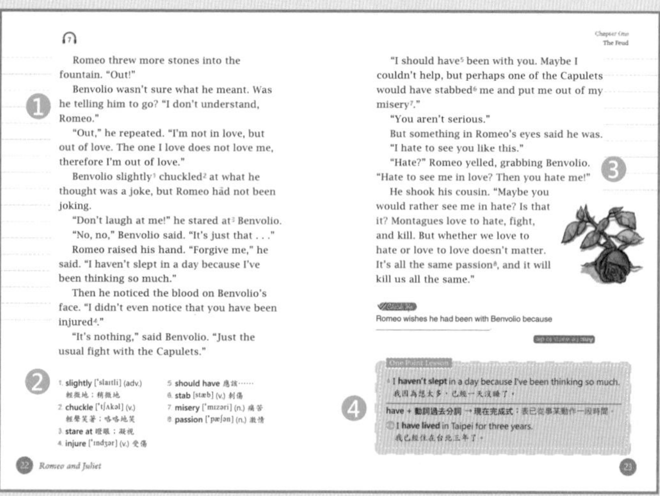

Chapter One
The Feud

Romeo threw more stones into the fountain. "Out!"

Benvolio wasn't sure what he meant. Was he telling him to go? "I don't understand, Romeo."

"Out," he repeated. "I'm not in love, but out of love. The one I love does not love me, therefore I'm out of love."

Benvolio slightly[1] chuckled[2] at what he thought was a joke, but Romeo had not been joking.

"Don't laugh at me!" he stared at[3] Benvolio.

"No, no," Benvolio said. "It's just that . . ."

Romeo raised his hand. "Forgive me," he said. "I haven't slept in a day because I've been thinking so much."

Then he noticed the blood on Benvolio's face. "I didn't even notice that you have been injured[4]."

"It's nothing," said Benvolio. "Just the usual fight with the Capulets."

1. **slightly** ['slaɪtli] (adv.) 輕微地；稍微地
2. **chuckle** ['tʃʌkəl] (v.) 輕聲笑著；咯咯地笑
3. **stare at** 瞪眼；凝視
4. **injure** ['ɪndʒər] (v.) 受傷
5. **should have** 應該……
6. **stab** [stæb] (v.) 刺傷
7. **misery** ['mɪzəri] (n.) 痛苦
8. **passion** ['pæʃən] (n.) 激情

22 *Romeo and Juliet*

"I should have[5] been with you. Maybe I couldn't help, but perhaps one of the Capulets would have stabbed[6] me and put me out of my misery[7]."

"You aren't serious."

But something in Romeo's eyes said he was.

"I hate to see you like this."

"Hate?" Romeo yelled, grabbing Benvolio. "Hate to see me in love? Then you hate me!"

He shook his cousin. "Maybe you would rather see me in hate? Is that it? Montagues love to hate, fight, and kill. But whether we love to hate or love to love doesn't matter. It's all the same passion[8], and it will kill us all the same."

Romeo wishes he had been with Benvolio because

One Point Lesson

I **haven't slept** in a day because I've been thinking so much.
我因為想太多，已經一天沒睡了。

have + 動詞過去分詞 → 現在完成式：表已從事某動作一段時間。

I **have lived** in Taipei for three years.
我已經住在台北三年了。

23

1 *Original English texts*

It is easy to understand the meaning of the text, because the text is rewritten according to the levels of the readers.

2 *Explanation of the vocabulary*

The words and expressions that include vocabulary above the elementary level are clearly defined.

3 *Response notes*

Spaces are included in the book so you can take notes about what you don't understand or what you want to remember.

4 *One point lesson*

In-depth analyses of major grammar points and expressions help you to understand sentences with difficult grammar.

Audio Recording

In the audio recording, native speakers narrate the texts in standard American English. By combining the written words and the audio recording, you can listen to English with great ease.

Audio books have been popular in Britain and America for many decades. They allow the listener to experience the proper word pronunciation and sentence intonation that add important meaning and drama to spoken English. Students will benefit from listening to the recording twenty or more times.

After you are familiar with the text and recording, listen once more with your eyes closed to check your listening comprehension. Finally, after you can listen with your eyes closed and understand every word and every sentence, you are then ready to mimic the native speaker.

Then you should make a recording by reading the text yourself. Then play both recordings to compare your oral skills with those of a native speaker.

Contents

Before You Read

Romeo

I live for the love of a woman, and Juliet is her name. There have been other women, but the memory of them has faded[1] from my mind. She is the one true love for me. Although I am a Montague, and she a Capulet, our love will overcome[2] the war between our families. Love is the most important thing in my life—actually, love is more important than life itself.

Juliet

Oh Romeo, Romeo, where are you Romeo? It seems that Fate[3] is designed to[4] keep me from my one and only true love. My father, Lord[5] Capulet, wants me to marry noble[6] Paris, but I cannot. As soon as I first saw him, I knew Romeo was the only man for me. I love Romeo more than my own life!

1. **fade** [feɪd] (v.) 退去；消失
2. **overcome** [ˌoʊvər'kʌm] (v.) 克服
3. **fate** [feɪt] (n.) 命運
4. **be designed to** 計畫將……
5. **lord** [lɔːrd] (n.) 勳爵；領主
6. **noble** ['noʊbəl] (n.) 貴族
7. **friar** ['fraɪr] (n.) （天主教）修士
8. **get married** 結婚

Friar[7] Lawrence

Children these days think too much about romance. Romeo and Juliet want to get married[8] ? They are too young! Their fathers hate each other! But maybe, just maybe, their marriage[9] may end the hate between their families.

Juliet's Nurse

I have cared for[10] Juliet for so long, that she is like a daughter to me. I must protect[11] her from Romeo, if he is not sincere in his love. However, if he is, he would make a fine husband for Juliet. He is the most handsome man I have ever seen!

Benvolio

I have many worries these days. It seems like fighting will break out[12] any day between my family, the Montagues, and my enemy[13], the Capulets. I am also worried about my cousin[14], Romeo. He is in love, and this has made him very sad. I will help him in any way to find his happiness.

9. **marriage** ['mærɪdʒ] (n.) 婚姻
10. **care for** 照料（顧）
11. **protect** [prə'tekt] (v.) 保護
12. **break out** 爆發；突然發生
13. **enemy** ['enəmi] (n.) 敵人
14. **cousin** ['kʌzən] (n.) 堂兄弟

Chapter One

The Feud[1]

"I will not fight," said Sampson, "but nobody should insult[2] me. If we see any Montagues, they had better be quiet."

"Or what?" asked Gregory.

"I'll kill them all."

"All?" Gregory stopped walking and looked at his friend.

"Every one of them," said Sampson. "If they are Montagues, then I'll fight them if they say something to me."

They began to walk on toward the square[3].

---

1. **feud** [fjuːd] (n.) 世仇
2. **insult** [ɪn'sʌlt] (v.) 侮辱
3. **square** [skwer] (n.) 廣場
4. **jokingly** ['dʒoʊkɪŋli] (adv.) 玩笑似地
5. **enemy** ['enəmi] (n.) 敵人
6. **explain** [ɪk'spleɪn] (v.) 解釋
7. **beat** [biːt] (v.) 打敗；勝過
8. **charm** [tʃɑːrm] (v.) 使陶醉；吸引
9. **be gone** 消失；不見

"What if one of the Montagues' dogs barks at you?" Gregory asked jokingly[4].

"Then I'd fight with it."

"What about women?"

This time Sampson stopped, as if to think about the question. "It's all the same. If they are Montagues, they are my enemies[5]. And they will know I'm angry."

"So you'd fight with the women?"

"I didn't say that," Sampson explained[6]. "I said they'd know I'm angry. I'd fight with the men. After beating[7] them, I would be kind to the women."

"You mean you'd charm[8] them? Once the Montague men were gone[9]?"

"Yes, I guess so."

"But that's not really showing them that you're angry. Unless you think charming the women is the same as fighting the men."

"Isn't it?" Sampson answered. "Either[1] way, it's about showing the Montagues who's the boss[2]. I'll beat the men with swords[3], the women with smiles and pretty words. It's all the same."

"I wish it were the same," said Gregory, seeing two servants[4] from the Montague family approaching[5] from across the square. "Then you could just smile and say kind things to these two and be satisfied[6]."

Sampson watched the two men strut[7] through the square. "I can think of nothing kind to say."

The two men began to walk toward Sampson and Gregory, looking at them with angry eyes. They were making nasty[8] remarks[9] among themselves about Sampson and Gregory.

Gregory gave an unnatural smile as the two passed by[10]. Sampson did the same, but he could not hold in[11] his hatred[12]. As soon as the men passed, he stuck out[13] his middle finger and went, "AARRRRRRR!"

1. **either** [ˈiːðər] (a.) 兩者中任一的
2. **boss** [bɒːs] (n.) 老大；長官
3. **sword** [sɔːrd] (n.) 劍
4. **servant** [ˈsɜːrvənt] (n.) 僕人
5. **approach** [əˈproʊtʃ] (v.) 接近
6. **satisfied** [ˈsætɪsfaɪd] (a.) 滿意的
7. **strut** [strʌt] (v.) 趾高氣昂地走
8. **nasty** [ˈnæsti] (a.) 下流的；卑鄙的
9. **remark** [rɪˈmɑːrk] (n.) 言辭
10. **pass by** 經過
11. **hold in** 抑制；約束 (hold-held-held)
12. **hatred** [ˈheɪtrɪd] (n.) 憎恨
13. **stick out** 伸出 (stick-stuck-stuck)

The men stopped and turned. "Are you giving us the finger, sir?" said one of them.

"Uh," Sampson whispered to Gregory, "is the law on our side if I say 'yes'?"

"No."

"Then, no," stated[1] Sampson.

"But I saw you stick out your finger," said the man named Abraham.

"And I heard you make a noise," said the other named[2] Balthasar.

"Then I stuck out my finger, sir," said Sampson innocently[3], "and I made a noise[4]. What about[5] it?"

"That's just like a man from the Capulet family, isn't it?" said the other man. "Making rude[6] gestures[7] to honest people. And then too cowardly[8] to confess to[9] it."

"Just like a Capulet," agreed Abraham. "Cowards[10]. Every one of them."

---

1. **state** [steɪt] (v.) 陳述；說明
2. **name** [neɪm] (v.) 被稱為
3. **innocently** [ˈɪnəsəntli] (adv.) 無辜地
4. **make a noise** 發出聲音
5. **What about . . . ?** ……認為如何？
6. **rude** [ruːd] (a.) 粗暴的
7. **gesture** [ˈdʒestʃər] (n.) 姿態
8. **cowardly** [ˈkaʊərdlɪ] (a.) 膽小的；怯懦的
9. **confess to** 承認
10. **coward** [ˈkaʊərd] (n.) 膽小鬼
11. **grab** [græb] (v.) 抓；取
12. **accidentally** [ˌæksɪˈdentli] (adv.) 意外地；偶然地
13. **wrestle** [ˈresəl] (v.) 搏鬥
14. **cheer** [tʃɪr] (v.) 歡呼；喝采

"There's no reason to call anyone a coward," said Gregory.

"I'll show you who's a coward!" said Sampson. As he grabbed[11] his knife, he accidentally[12] pushed Gregory into Abraham.

"You saw that, Balthasar? He attacked me," shouted Abraham.

It was too late to keep the peace. All four men wrestled[13] in the street. A crowd gathered and began shouting and cheering[14].

Check Up

What did the Montague men say about the Capulet men?

- a Capulets liked to break the law.
- b Caputlets were cowards.
- c Capulets were innocent.

Ans: b

Benvolio, Old Montague's nephew[1], heard the fighting. He didn't really like the feud between his family and the Capulets. He knew that all this hatred would only result in[2] death, and death in more hatred.

But he knew the only way to stop the fighting was to jump between the angry men. Therefore, he drew[3] his sword and ran toward the four men fighting in the square.

"Peace! Put your weapons[4] away[5]!" Benvolio shouted, as he pulled the men off[6] each other.

A tall man walked forward. He pulled out his sword and touched the point[7].

It was Tybalt, Capulet's nephew, an arrogant[8] man of thirty. He was very arrogant, but he was also the best swordsman[9] in Verona.

---

1. **nephew** [ˈnefjuː] (n.) 姪子
2. **result in** 導致
3. **draw** [drɔː] (v.) 拔出
4. **weapon** [ˈwepən] (n.) 武器
5. **put . . . away** 收好
6. **pull off** 拉開
7. **point** [pɔɪnt] (n.) 尖端
8. **arrogant** [ˈærəgənt] (a.) 傲慢的
9. **swordsman** [ˈsɔːrdzmən] (n.) 劍客
10. **twisted** [ˈtwɪstɪd] (a.) 古怪的
11. **barely** [ˈberli] (adv.) 幾乎沒有
12. **defend oneself** 自我防衛
13. **lunge at** 撲；衝；刺

"Tybalt," said Benvolio. "Put your sword away. I'm trying to keep the peace. Please help me."

"Peace? You stand there with your sword in your hand talking of peace?" Tybalt spoke with a twisted[10] smile.

Benvolio barely[11] had time to defend himself[12] before Tybalt lunged at[13] him.

The crowd cheered again. "Kill the Montagues!" yelled some.

"Kill the Capulets!" others yelled.

"Kill them all!" yelled more.

Check Up

Benvolio wanted to stop the men from fighting because __________.

a he thought the Montague men would lose

b he didn't want someone to die

Ans: b

"Kill the Capulets?" murmured[1] an old man who was walking out of[2] a nearby church.

It was Capulet, holding on to his young wife's arm. "Give me my sword!"

"Sword?" his wife scolded[3]. "You need a cane[4], not a sword."

"I know it's Capulet!" Another old man hobbled[5] across the square. It was Montague. "Lead me over to him." he said.

"How can you fight? You can barely walk!" said Lady Montague.

Then the crowd went silent as some horses neared. Escalus, the Prince of Verona, and his soldiers rode toward them. He circled[6] Tybalt and Benvolio. The onlookers[7] hurried off[8].

1. **murmur** [ˈmɜːrmər] (v.) 低聲說
2. **out of** 從……出來
3. **scold** [skoʊld] (v.) 責罵
4. **cane** [keɪn] (n.) 拐杖
5. **hobble** [ˈhɑːbəl] (v.) 跛行
6. **circle** [ˈsɜːrkəl] (v.) 圍著
7. **onlooker** [ˈɑːnˌlʊkər] (n.) 旁觀者
8. **hurry off** 匆忙離去
9. **rebel** [ˈrebəl] (n.) 反叛者；造反者
10. **roar** [rɔːr] (v.) 吼叫
11. **command** [kəˈmænd] (v.) 命令
12. **responsible** [rɪˈspɑːnsəbəl] (a.) 負責的
13. **be supposed to** 應該

"Rebels[9]!" roared[10] the prince. "Throw your weapons to the ground!"

Tybalt and Benvolio did as the prince commanded[11].

"Now," Escalus said, "where are the people responsible[12]? I'm talking about the two older men, Capulet and Montague."

He searched the streets and found the two old men. "You, Capulet, and you, Montague, stand in front of me!"

The two old men came forward. "You are leaders in this city and are supposed to[13] be moral[14]. But instead of teaching the people how to be noble, you force them to participate in your pointless feud. Well, I've been patient for too long."

He drew his sword. "If your feud ever disturbs[15] the streets again, you both will pay for[16] it with your lives! Do you understand?"

They both nodded[17].

14. **moral** [ˈmɔːrəl] (a.) 講道德的
15. **disturb** [dɪˈstɜːrb] (v.) 擾亂
16. **pay for** 為……付出代價 (pay-paid-paid)
17. **nod** [nɑːd] (v.) 點頭 (nod-nodded-nodded)

When Montague's people returned to their palace[1], Lady Montague spoke to Benvolio,

"My Romeo wasn't in this fight, was he?"

"No," said Benvolio, "If Romeo wasn't with you, then where is he?"

"The last time I saw him, madam, was this morning. He was lying on the garden wall, and he looked so sad."

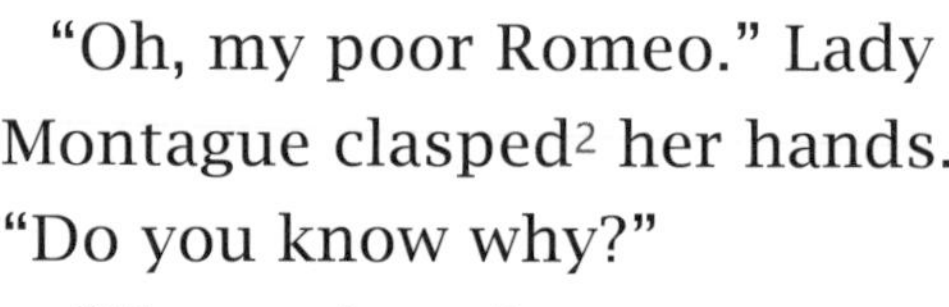

"Oh, my poor Romeo." Lady Montague clasped[2] her hands. "Do you know why?"

"No, madam. I went over to him, but he ran away[3]."

"I also have seen him in the garden looking sad. I've asked him why, but he said nothing to me." Lady Montague smiled sadly.

As they reached the palace, a young man stepped out of the rose bushes[4].

1. **palace** [ˈpælɪs] (n.) 皇宮
2. **clasp** [klæsp] (v.) 緊握
3. **run away** 跑掉
4. **bush** [bʊʃ] (n.) 灌木叢
5. **pat** [pæt] (v.) 輕拍 (pat-patted-patted)
6. **wrist** [rɪst] (n.) 手腕
7. **toss** [tɒːs] (v.) 扔；拋
8. **fountain** [ˈfaʊntən] (n.) 噴泉

"There's Romeo, now, madam," said Benvolio. "Should I talk to him again?"

"Please," said Lady Montague. She patted[5] Benvolio's wrist[6] and left with her husband.

"Good morning, cousin," said Benvolio.

"Is it still morning?" said Romeo, tossing[7] a stone into the fountain[8].

"It is only nine o'clock."

"Sad hours pass slowly." Romeo threw another stone.

"Why do the hours seem so long?"

"I don't have anything to make them short."

"You mean love," said Benvolio happily. "I thought you might be in love!"

True or False.

a Romeo ran away from his home. ____

b Romeo seems to be very depressed these days. ____

c Benvolio thinks Romeo is in love. ____

7

Romeo threw more stones into the fountain. "Out!"

Benvolio wasn't sure what he meant. Was he telling him to go? "I don't understand, Romeo."

"Out," he repeated. "I'm not in love, but out of love. The one I love does not love me, therefore I'm out of love."

Benvolio slightly[1] chuckled[2] at what he thought was a joke, but Romeo had not been joking.

"Don't laugh at me!" he stared at[3] Benvolio.

"No, no," Benvolio said. "It's just that . . ."

Romeo raised his hand. "Forgive me," he said. "I haven't slept in a day because I've been thinking so much."

Then he noticed the blood on Benvolio's face. "I didn't even notice that you have been injured[4]."

"It's nothing," said Benvolio. "Just the usual fight with the Capulets."

1. **slightly** [ˈslaɪtli] (adv.) 輕微地；稍微地
2. **chuckle** [ˈtʃʌkəl] (v.) 輕聲笑著；咯咯地笑
3. **stare at** 瞪眼；凝視
4. **injure** [ˈɪndʒər] (v.) 受傷
5. **should have** 應該……
6. **stab** [stæb] (v.) 刺傷
7. **misery** [ˈmɪzəri] (n.) 痛苦
8. **passion** [ˈpæʃən] (n.) 激情

"I should have[5] been with you. Maybe I couldn't help, but perhaps one of the Capulets would have stabbed[6] me and put me out of my misery[7]."

"You aren't serious."

But something in Romeo's eyes said he was.

"I hate to see you like this."

"Hate?" Romeo yelled, grabbing Benvolio. "Hate to see me in love? Then you hate me!"

He shook his cousin. "Maybe you would rather see me in hate? Is that it? Montagues love to hate, fight, and kill. But whether we love to hate or love to love doesn't matter. It's all the same passion[8], and it will kill us all the same."

Check Up

Romeo wishes he had been with Benvolio because ______________________.

Ans: he wants to die

One Point Lesson

I **haven't slept** in a day because I've been thinking so much.
我因為想太多，已經一天沒睡了。

have + 動詞過去分詞 → 現在完成式：表已從事某動作一段時間。

e.g. I **have lived** in Taipei for three years.
我已經住在台北三年了。

8

Benvolio didn't like what Romeo had said. After all, he had risked[1] his life to stop a fight earlier. But he knew that Romeo was right and that the problem with the family was because of excessive[2] passion. He also knew that Romeo possessed[3] that same passion. He wanted to help his cousin.

"Can you tell me who it is that you love?"

"A woman," he mumbled[4].

"Yes," said Benvolio, "Who?"

"Rosaline," said Romeo.

"Rosaline?" Benvolio brightened[5]. "Things may be alright. I know she will be at a party in the Capulet's house tonight."

"In the Capulet's house? My father's enemy? I cannot enter the Capulet's house. I will surely be killed, although that may not be so bad."

"Cousin," said Benvolio. "Mercutio, one of our friends, is invited to the party. We can go with him. We will wear masks, so no one will recognize[6] us."

---

1. **risk** [rɪsk] (v.) 冒……風險
2. **excessive** [ɪk'sesɪv] (a.) 過度的
3. **possess** [pə'zes] (v.) 擁有
4. **mumble** ['mʌmbəl] (v.) 喃喃自語
5. **brighten** ['braɪtn] (v.) 變明亮
6. **recognize** ['rekəgnaɪz] (v.) 認出

Romeo looked up happily.

"Not ready to die yet, eh?" Benvolio was glad to see Romeo look a little happier. "But I warn you: there will be so many pretty girls there that you will forget about Rosaline."

"Oh, Benvolio. There is no one more beautiful than her. And I would not want another."

"Believe what you want," said Benvolio. "Just get ready for the party."

Check Up

What is Benvolio's plan to make Romeo feel better?

a He will introduce Romeo to another, more beautiful girl.

b He will take Romeo on a short vacation.

c He will take Romeo to a party where he can meet his love.

Ans: c

9

Capulet, drinking some cool water, leaned[1] back in his chair. "I'm glad that Montague has to follow the same rules as me. Both of us will die if either of us breaks the peace." He laughed. "Break the peace! That's funny!"

"Why?" asked Capulet's kinsman[2], Paris.

"Because the two of us are too old to break the peace. Old men like us should be able to stay out of a fight."

"That's true, sir, but what about your young kinsmen? They don't always think clearly when they are angry."

"Yes," said Capulet, "the young think with their hearts and not their heads. But they will listen to their elders[3]."

"Let's hope so," said Paris. "You both are such gentlemen. I can't believe this quarrel[4] has continued for so long."

"Truly, and I think I've even forgotten how it started." Capulet laughed again.

Paris laughed with him, but he wanted to change the subject[5]. "Have you thought about my request[6]?"

"Your request? I had almost forgotten," said Capulet.

1. **lean** [liːn] (v.) 倚靠
2. **kinsman** [ˈkɪnzmən] (n.) （男性）親屬
3. **elder** [ˈeldər] (n.) 年長者
4. **quarrel** [ˈkwɔːrəl] (n.) 爭吵
5. **subject** [ˈsʌbdʒɪkt] (n.) 話題
6. **request** [rɪˈkwest] (n.) 請求

Check Up

Short answer question.

According to Capulet, what do young men think with?

____

Ans: They think with their hearts.

10

"Are you opposed to[1] the marriage?" asked Paris.

"No," answered Capulet, "though I'm not really for it[2] either. You are a fine young man, but Juliet is so young. Give her two more years."

"Many ladies younger than her are already mothers," Paris gently[3] objected[4].

"Because they married too soon!" snapped[5] Capulet.

But he knew that Paris was right. His wife was Juliet's age when they married. But Capulet wasn't ready to see his only daughter get married. However, there was no reason why she shouldn't get married. After all, she couldn't stay his little girl forever.

"I think I have upset[6] you," said Paris. "You are her father, and you know what is best for her."

"Wait," said Capulet.

Paris stopped.

1. **be opposed to** 反對
2. **for it** 贊成；支持
3. **gently** ['dʒentli] (adv.) 小心地；有教養地；高貴地
4. **object** [əb'dʒekt] (v.) 反對
5. **snap** [snæp] (v.) 厲聲說
6. **upset** [ʌp'set] (v.) 使心煩 (upset-upset-upset)
7. **blessing** ['blesɪŋ] (n.) 祝福

"I will agree to the marriage," said Capulet. "But the final decision is hers. Come to the party tonight. If she agrees to marry you, then you will have my blessing[7]."

"Thank you. I will!" cried Paris, as he walked out of the room.

Alone, Capulet looked out the window. He imagined Juliet falling in love, just as he had done. Then he went to sleep.

One Point Lesson

He imagined Juliet falling in love, just as he **had done.**
他想像茱麗葉墜入愛河，就和他以前一樣。

had + 動詞過去分詞
→ **過去完成式**：表示某動作發生於過去某時間點前

e.g. When I got to the stop, the bus **had** just **left**.
當我到公車站時，車子已經走了。

Understanding the Story

The Streets of Verona

In "Romeo and Juliet", Shakespeare paints a picture of fourteenth century Verona as a city where armed[1] men fight old family feuds in the streets. True to this image, Verona was a town being torn apart[2] by politics[3] over centuries. In 1158, Verona was caught up in civil war[4]. Many noble[5] families in Verona were loyal to the Catholic[6] Pope[7]. However, many other nobles were loyal to the Holy Roman Emperor[8], Freidrich Barbarossa.

Although the "ancient feud" between the Montagues and the Capulets is never explained in Shakespeare's play, it probably dates back this conflict[9], which was over 200 years old at the time of Romeo and Juliet. These feuds would involve not only the leaders, but the sons, daughters, cousins and even servants of each family.

The fact that many noble families in Verona were hostile[10] to one another is evident[11] even today. Visitors to Verona can find hundreds of old houses with thick walls and fortified[12] entrances. These buildings are left over from the time when armed men, similar to Tybalt and Mercutio, roamed[13] the streets of Verona.

It is romantic to think that the tragic love affair between Romeo and Juliet ended these feuds, but their story, unlike the historical background, is pure fiction[14].

---

1. **armed** [ɑːrmd] (a.) 武裝的
2. **torn apart** 不安
3. **politics** [ˈpɑːlətɪks] (n.) 政治
4. **civil war** 內戰
5. **noble** [ˈnoʊbəl] (a.) 貴族的
6. **Catholic** [ˈkæθəlɪk] (a.) 天主教的
7. **Pope** [poʊp] (n.) 羅馬天主教教皇
8. **emperor** [ˈempərə(r)] (n.) 皇帝
9. **conflict** [ˈkɑːnflɪkt] (n.) 衝突
10. **hostile** [ˈhɑːstəl] (a.) 敵意的
11. **evident** [ˈevɪdənt] (a.) 明顯的
12. **fortified** [ˈfɔːrtɪfaɪd] (a.) 加強防禦的
13. **roam** [roʊm] (v.) 漫步
14. **fiction** [ˈfɪkʃən] (n.) 虛構

Chapter Two

11 Love at First Sight[1]

"Nurse!" called Lady Capulet.

"Coming, madam," yelled the nurse as she ran down the stairs.

"Where's my daughter?" demanded[2] Lady Capulet.

"My ladybird! Where are you, Juliet!" the nurse shouted up the stairs.

Juliet appeared[3] at the top of the stairs. Her long, black hair looked beautiful.

"Now," began Lady Capulet, "you are old enough to get married. So tell me, Juliet, how would you like to be married?"

Juliet thought the question was awkward[4]. She didn't want to defy[5] her mother, so she chose her words carefully. "I've always dreamed of getting married," she said politely[6]. "But I'm still too young to think of marriage."

Lady Capulet knew this would be difficult, so she spoke directly. "I will be brief. The brave[7] Paris wants to marry you. What do you think, Juliet?" spoke Lady Capulet. "He will be at the party tonight. Take a good look at him before you answer."

"I will look," replied Juliet.

Lady Capulet couldn't tell[8] if Juliet was happy and wondered if she could love Paris.

1. **at first sight** 第一眼
2. **demand** [dɪˈmænd] (v.) 查問
3. **appear** [əˈpɪr] (v.) 出現
4. **awkward** [ˈɒːkwərd] (a.) 棘手的
5. **defy** [dɪˈfaɪ] (v.) 當面反抗 (defy-defied-defied)
6. **politely** [pəˈlaɪtli] (adv.) 委婉地
7. **brave** [breɪv] (a.) 勇敢的
8. **tell** [tel] (v.) 辨別

One Point Lesson

"Coming, madam," yelled the nurse **as** she ran down the stairs.
「夫人，我來了。」奶媽一邊跑下樓梯，一邊叫著。

as：（介系詞）以……的身分；像，如同
（連接詞）當……時；依照

e.g. Just do it **as** I say. 照我說的做。

"Come on, come on!" yelled Mercutio to Romeo and Benvolio. "We're going to be late."

"I thought a man in love could fly here on Cupid's wings," Mercutio laughed.

"You're wrong, Mercutio," Romeo said. "Love is burdensome[1], so a lover's feet are slow."

"Does that mean you can't dance tonight?" Mercutio asked. "If I was in love, I would dance."

"Well, we don't have time to talk. We are already late. I'm sure we've missed dinner, and we'll miss the dance if we don't hurry," said Benvolio.

"It's okay if we are late," said Romeo. "I fear tonight will be a disaster[2]."

"Okay," said Mercutio. "We'd better hurry then. I don't want to keep a man in love from his disaster!"

They hurried down the street and arrived at a gate. Just beyond[3] was a large hall, and they could hear the sounds of music and laughter[4].

"Let's put on our disguises[5]," said Mercutio. "Otherwise[6], the doorman[7] will not let us enter since we are Montagues."

The three entered the party wearing masks. Mercutio and Benvolio joined the dance while Romeo walked among the crowd of people. He was hoping to see his beloved[8] Rosaline.

1. **burdensome** [ˈbɜːrdnsəm] (a.) 惱人的；繁重的
2. **disaster** [dɪˈzæstər] (n.) 災難
3. **beyond** [bɪˈjɑːnd] (prep.) 在……的那一邊
4. **laughter** [ˈlæftər] (n.) 笑聲
5. **disguise** [dɪsˈgaɪz] (n.) 偽裝
6. **otherwise** [ˈʌðərwaɪz] (adv.) 否則
7. **doorman** [ˈdɔːrmæn] (n.) 門房
8. **beloved** [bɪˈlʌvɪd] (a.) 心愛的

13

But Romeo saw someone else. She seemed like a picture. She moved effortlessly[1], as if she was floating[2] on air. She was so beautiful. She was like an angel.

"She is so beautiful that she makes the stars shine[3] bright," Romeo mumbled to himself.

He walked as if in a trance[4]. Was I really in love before now? he asked himself.

"No," he answered aloud. "No, I have never really seen beauty before tonight."

He lifted his mask, hoping the lady would see his face. She did.

"What's the matter?" asked Paris, as Juliet stopped dancing.

"Nothing," she answered. "Something is in my eye."

They continued dancing, but Juliet couldn't stop looking at the person she had just seen.

1. **effortlessly** [ˈefərtləsli] (adv.) 輕鬆地；毫不費力地
2. **float** [floʊt] (v.) 漂浮；飄動
3. **shine** [ʃaɪn] (v.) 閃耀；發光
4. **trance** [træns] (n.) 恍惚

Neither could her cousin. "I know that face," Tybalt thought. He couldn't quite remember where he had seen him, but he thought he looked like a fine gentleman.

He continued to stare, and he slowly remembered where he had seen him. It was in the square. Tybalt became angry.

"Get my sword!" growled[5] Tybalt to his servant.

The servant did what he was told.

"A Montague!" Tybalt said angrily. "He comes to our party masked[6]. To make fun of[7] us!"

5. **growl** [graʊl] (v.) 咆哮
6. **masked** [mæskt] (a.) 戴面具的
7. **make fun of** 嘲弄

14

"What's the matter?" asked Capulet, as he walked over to Tybalt.

"Uncle," said Tybalt, pointing to Romeo, "he is a Montague."

Capulet looked. "It's young Romeo."

"Romeo!" shouted Tybalt.

"Calm down[1], nephew," said Capulet. "Leave him alone[2]. He appears to[3] be a gentleman. Be patient, and don't think about him."

"Too late," replied Tybalt.

Capulet didn't like that Tybalt was being rude, but he tried to reason with[4] him.

"It's what I want," he said. "Please respect[5] my wishes, and be happy. Sad people don't belong at parties."

"Sad people belong at parties when an enemy is a guest. I cannot tolerate[6] him."

"You will tolerate him!" Capulet scolded.

1. **calm down** 冷靜下來
2. **leave *A* alone** 避免打擾A
3. **appear to** 似乎；看來好像
4. **reason (with)** 勸說
5. **respect** [rɪ'spekt] (v.) 尊重
6. **tolerate** ['tɑːləreɪt] (v.) 容忍
7. **spin** [spɪn] (v.) 使旋轉 (spin-spun-spun)
8. **mutter** ['mʌtər] (v.) 低聲嘀咕
9. **musician** [mjʊ'zɪʃən] (n.) 演奏者

Tybalt turned his back on his uncle.

"How can you turn your back on me?" shouted Capulet, grabbing Tybalt and spinning[7] him around. "I'm the master here, and I said to leave him alone."

"It's terrible," muttered[8] Tybalt.

"It is, but you're being childish," said Capulet.

"Childish? I'm thirty years old," answered Tybalt.

"Will you be a man if you cause trouble with my guests?"

Their voices became loud. The musicians[9] stopped playing and the guests stopped dancing.

15

"Excuse me, my lady," said Paris to Juliet. "If I'm to be your husband, what your family does affects[1] me. I had better see what the problem is."

"Of course," answered Juliet, but she didn't even hear what he said. It was good that he was leaving, though.

Capulet noticed that they were being too loud.

"There's nothing to be concerned about[2]. Please continue dancing and having fun," he declared[3]. Then he pinched[4] Tybalt's cheek and told him to go and dance.

Tybalt pretended[5] that it was nothing. He bowed to his uncle and walked away bitterly[6].

On the dance floor, Juliet heard a whisper in her ear. "The dancing is starting," it said. "But follow me."

"Where to?" She turned and saw Romeo. Even with a mask on, he was the most handsome man she had ever seen.

She followed him to a private[7] spot[8]. Romeo removed[9] his mask and took Juliet's hand.

"Your hands are gentle," he said. "You are like an angel, and I would like to give you a tender[10] kiss."

Juliet felt excited as the blood rushed to her head, but she kept calm. "Angels have wings and often fly away," she said. Then she gently laced[11] her fingers through his and held his hands tightly[12].

Romeo shivered[13]. The sensation[14] of her touch was amazing. He wanted to kiss her more than ever, but she hadn't given him permission[15].

---

1. **affect** [ə'fekt] (v.) 影響
2. **concerned about** 擔憂
3. **declare** [dɪ'kler] (v.) 宣告
4. **pinch** [pɪntʃ] (v.) 捏
5. **pretend** [prɪ'tend] (v.) 假裝
6. **bitterly** ['bɪtərli] (adv.) 不痛快地
7. **private** ['praɪvɪt] (a.) 隱蔽的
8. **spot** [spɑːt] (n.) 地點
9. **remove** [rɪ'muːv] (v.) 移開
10. **tender** ['tendər] (a.) 溫柔的
11. **lace** [les] (v.) 手穿過……
12. **tightly** ['taɪtli] (adv.) 緊地
13. **shiver** ['ʃɪvər] (v.) 發抖
14. **sensation** [sen'seɪʃən] (n.) 感覺
15. **permission** [pər'mɪʃən] (n.) 允許

"Don't angels have lips?" he said as he stroked[1] her hand.

"Yes," she said. She knew Romeo wanted to kiss her, and she wanted him to. But she didn't want to be too bold[2]. Juliet knew it wasn't proper[3] for a young lady to tell a stranger to kiss her. But his touch was so gentle, so strong, and so warm that she could almost imagine what his lips would feel like.

How could she get him to kiss her? Romeo was waiting for an answer. Juliet turned her eyes away[4] because she was afraid he would know how she felt.

"I guess your lips don't desire a kiss," he said as he began to release[5] her hand.

But Juliet wouldn't let go. She moved Romeo's hand to her heart.

Romeo felt Juliet's heart pounding[6]. She looked so amazing that he felt like he would melt away[7] if their lips touched. Yet Romeo couldn't believe what he did next.

He kissed her.

"Madam!" yelled the nurse, pushing her way toward them. "Madam, your father and Paris are looking for you."

Juliet stepped away[8], still staring at Romeo.

Romeo put his mask back on. "Who is her father?"

1. **stroke** [stroʊk] (v.)（用手）摸
2. **bold** [boʊld] (a.) 大膽的
3. **proper** [ˈprɑːpər] (a.) 適當的
4. **turn away** 移走
5. **release** [rɪˈliːs] (v.) 鬆開
6. **pound** [paʊnd] (v.) 心劇跳
7. **melt away** 融化
8. **step away** 跨開 (step-stepped-stepped)

Who interrupted Romeo and Juliet?

a Lord Capulet　b the nurse　c Benvolio

Ans: b

The nurse recognized Romeo. “This is Juliet and her father is the owner of this house.”

“She is a Capulet?” said Romeo.

“As you are a . . .”

“A bachelor[1] !” interrupted[2] Benvolio. “Come,” he whispered. “We’ve been discovered[3]. We have to leave before there is trouble.”

“There is already trouble,” said Romeo.

1. **bachelor** ['bætʃələr] (n.) 單身漢
2. **interrupt** [ˌɪntə'rʌpt] (v.) 打斷
3. **discover** [dɪs'kʌvər] (v.) 發現
4. **might as well** 該……做
5. **deeply** ['di:pli] (adv.) 強烈地

"Who . . . who was that gentleman?" asked Juliet.

"The most handsome man I've ever seen," answered the nurse.

"Is he married?" asked Juliet.

"No, but he might as well[4] be."

Juliet stared at the nurse. "What do you mean?"

"His name is Romeo Montague. The only son of your great enemy."

"Of course, he would have to be a Montague," said Juliet.

She didn't explain but thought deeply[5] of Romeo. She knew right then that her whole world had just changed. She could no longer live in her old world, the one without Romeo.

That Romeo was her enemy only made her feelings stronger. She knew at that moment that the world, and not her love, would have to change. It was simple.

"So," she said, "my only love has come from my only hate."

"What's this? Love?" whispered the nurse. "My baby girl is in love?"

"Juliet!" came a call in the distance. It was Paris or her father. Juliet didn't care.

"Tell them I've gone to bed."

A Choose the correct answers.

ⓐ Capulet ⓑ Benvolio ⓒ Paris ⓓ Tybalt

1. Who tried to stop the fight in the square? ________
2. Who is Capulet's nephew and an arrogant man? ________
3. Who was having the party? ________
4. Who asked to be married to Juliet? ________

B True or False.

T F 1. The Capulets and the Montagues were having a feud.

T F 2. Romeo participated in the fight in the square.

T F 3. If there is another fight, the prince will kill Capulet and Montague.

T F 4. Escalus stopped the fight in the square.

T F 5. Romeo was upset because he hated the Capulets.

C Choose the correct answers.

1. What happened between Romeo and Juliet during the party?

   (a) Romeo got into a fight.
   (b) They fell in love at first sight.
   (c) They had an argument.

2. What did Capulet want at the party?

   (a) He wanted Tybalt to leave Romeo alone.
   (b) He wanted Romeo to dance with Juliet.
   (c) He wanted Paris to fight Romeo.

D Rearrange the sentences in chronological order.

1. Romeo meets Juliet.
2. Romeo goes to the party.
3. Paris dances with Juliet.
4. Lady Capulet tells Juliet to marry Paris.
5. The music at the party stops.

_____ ⇨ _____ ⇨ _____ ⇨ _____ ⇨ _____

18

The Secret Wedding

Romeo was thinking strange thoughts. He couldn't go home. He needed to see Juliet again, but he could not go to her house. Yet there was nowhere[1] else to go.

He walked in the night back to the house of his father's enemy. He climbed the garden wall and waited. He crouched[2] in the bushes.

1. **nowhere** [ˈnoʊwer] (adv.) 無處地；沒有地方地
2. **crouch** [kraʊtʃ] (v.) 蹲
3. **onto** [ˈɑːntuː] (prep.) 到……之上
4. **gasp** [gæsp] (v.) 倒抽一口氣
5. **set** [set] (v.) 置；放
6. **breathing** [ˈbriːðɪŋ] (n.) 呼吸；氣音

In an upper room, lit by a single candle, was the shadow of a woman.

"What light is in the window," whispered Romeo.

The door slowly opened, and Juliet stepped onto[3] the balcony.

"It is my angel," gasped[4] Romeo, "Oh, it is my love! Oh, if only she knew how much I loved her."

Juliet carried a candle and set[5] it on the balcony. She looked into the darkness, and her lips moved.

"She speaks," whispered Romeo,

Then she spoke. "Ah, me!"

"Oh, speak again, my angel," said Romeo softly.

He could see her breathing[6]. He wanted to run to her, climb up the balcony, and hold her. But he feared that once she knew his name, she would hate him.

Where did Romeo go that night?

a Go to sleep, and he dreamed a strange dream.

b Go back to his house with his friends.

c Go to hide in the garden of his enemy's house.

Ans: c

19

Juliet spoke again, "Oh, Romeo, Romeo, where are you, my sweet Romeo? Forget that you are a Montague. If not, just say you love me, and I'll no longer be a Capulet."

Romeo fell backward. Had he died? Was this heaven[1]? He stood and looked. Juliet was still there.

"It is only your name that is my enemy," Juliet said. "What's a Montague? It's only a name. And a rose would smell just as sweet if it was given another name. Romeo, forget your name, and be only mine."

Romeo couldn't endure[2] it anymore.

"I will be only yours!" he cried, coming forward. "Just be my love, and I will never be Romeo."

"Who's there?" said Juliet, stepping back.

"I don't know how to tell you who I am," said Romeo. "I hate my name because it is the name of your enemy."

1. **heaven** [ˈhevən] (n.) 天堂
2. **endure** [ɪnˈdʊr] (v.) 忍受
3. **miserably** [ˈmɪzərəbəli] (adv.) 悲慘地

"I haven't heard you speak much, but I know the sound. You are Romeo, and a Montague. How did you get here?" she demanded, "and why? The walls are high and hard to climb. And it's dangerous if anyone finds you here."

"It was because of love that I jumped over the walls. And a person can do anything for love."

Love! Romeo had said love. She wanted him to say it again, but she was afraid.

"I'm afraid someone will find you here."

"Let them find me," said Romeo. "I would rather die here with you than live miserably[3] without your love."

She closed her eyes and imagined him.
"Do you love me?" she whispered.

"I love you more than words can say!" answered Romeo.

20

"Madam!" came a voice from within the house. It was the nurse.

Juliet's eyes opened wide. "A noise. Go, dear love!"

Romeo began to tiptoe[1] away, but Juliet didn't want him to leave. "No, stay!"

Juliet leaned[2] over the balcony. "What can I do to make you happy?"

"You can give me your heart, and I will give you mine."

"I gave it to you before you asked," she said. Juliet smiled. "My love is boundless[3] and as deep as the sea. The more I give to you, the more I have."

"My lady!" shouted the nurse.

"In a minute!" yelled Juliet.

Then, to Romeo, she said, "If your love is real and you want to marry me, please tell me."

"I do want to marry you," said Romeo.

"When?"

"Tomorrow," promised Romeo boldly[4]. "I'll come myself."

"No," said Juliet, "it's too dangerous. I'll send my nurse. When will you be ready?"

"By . . . by nine o'clock tomorrow."

"It will seem like twenty years till then," she said, "but I will endure it. Go now."

Romeo stepped away.

She blew a kiss[5]. "Good night, good night. Parting[6] is always sweet sorrow[7], but I will see you tomorrow."

He could almost feel her kiss touch his lips. "I will not sleep until then," he said, and then disappeared into the night.

---

1. **tiptoe** [ˈtɪptoʊ] (v.) 躡手躡腳地走
2. **lean** [liːn] (v.) 傾身；倚靠
3. **boundless** [ˈbaʊndləs] (a.) 無窮的
4. **boldly** [ˈboʊldli] (adv.) 大膽地
5. **blow a kiss** 給……飛吻 (blow-blew-blown)
6. **parting** [ˈpɑːrtɪŋ] (n.) 【書】告別
7. **sorrow** [ˈsɑːroʊ] (n.) 悲傷

Friar[1] Lawrence was working in the garden. "Ahh!" he breathed in the smell of fresh flowers. "The earth[2] is a wonderful thing," he thought. "It gives life to new flowers and trees."

He pulled a pair of scissors from his pocket and began to prune[3] the flowers, humming as he worked.

"Good morning, Father," came an urgent[4] voice.

Friar Lawrence turned and saw Romeo. "My boy," he said, "what are you doing up so early in the morning? I've never known a young man to wake up so early."

He smiled warmly. "Or maybe you did not go to bed last night?"

"I didn't go to bed, but I got the sweetest rest anyway."

"Were you with Rosaline and resting without sleeping?" Friar Lawrence asked.

"Rosaline? I have forgotten all about her."

"That's good, my son, but then where were you?"

"Dancing with my enemy!" Romeo exclaimed[5]. "That's where I forgot about Rosaline and learned what true love is."

Friar Lawrence rubbed his eyes.

"You're confusing[6] me, Romeo," he said. "Speak directly."

"I love Capulet's daughter," said Romeo. "And she loves me. We've just met, but our love is everlasting[7]. We have sworn[8] to marry. You must marry us today."

"Marry you!" Friar Lawrence shook his head. "You cried for Rosaline only yesterday. Now you say you will marry another?"

---

1. **friar** [ˈfraɪər] (n.) 修士
2. **earth** [ɜːrθ] (n.) 土；泥
3. **prune** [pruːn] (v.) 修剪
4. **urgent** [ˈɜːrdʒənt] (a.) 緊急的
5. **exclaim** [ɪkˈskleɪm] (v.) 驚呼
6. **confuse** [kənˈfjuːz] (v.) 使困惑
7. **everlasting** [ˌevərˈlæstɪŋ] (a.) 永遠的
8. **swear** [swer] (v.) 發誓

Check Up

What does Friar Lawrence probably think about Romeo?

a Romeo is very faithful to Rosaline.

b Romeo falls in and out of love too easily.

c Romeo is very wise.

Ans: b

22

"Didn't you scold me for loving Rosaline?"

"I scolded you for idolizing[1] her."

"Didn't you tell me not to love her?"

"Yes, but not to fall in love again so quickly. You are too passionate[2]."

"Don't we all live by passion?"

"We live by reason[3]," insisted Friar Lawrence. "We die by our passions."

"Well then praise me for being reasonable[4]. I now know you were right about Rosaline. I wasn't in love with her. But Juliet is perfect, and it's reasonable to love perfection[5], right? You must marry us."

Friar Lawrence looked out at the sunrise. He couldn't believe what he was hearing. How could he marry someone so young and naive[6]? And without the parents' consent[7]?

1. **idolize** ['aɪdəlaɪz] (v.) 極度崇拜
2. **passionate** ['pæʃənɪt] (a.) 激情的
3. **reason** ['riːzən] (n.) 理性
4. **reasonable** ['riːzənəbəl] (a.) 有理性的
5. **perfection** [pər'fekʃən] (n.) 完美的人
6. **naive** [naɪ'iːv] (a.) 天真的
7. **consent** [kən'sent] (n.) 同意
8. **impatiently** [ɪm'peɪʃəntli] (adv.) 沒耐心地
9. **persuade** [pər'sweɪd] (v.) 說服

"Father?" asked Romeo impatiently[8].

The friar didn't answer. He continued thinking. Maybe a marriage would force peace between the fighting families.

"You have not persuaded[9] me, Romeo," said Friar Lawrence at last, "but I will marry you. And I hope this marriage brings love to your two families instead of hate."

Friar Lawrence put his scissors back into his pocket and led Romeo to the church.

23

"Where is Romeo?" Mercutio leaned against the church steps. "You said he wasn't home when you got there."

"No," answered Benvolio, "but Tybalt has sent a letter to him."

"A challenge to fight?" asked Mercutio.

Benvolio kicked a stone. "I'm sure Romeo will accept the challenge[1]."

"Then Romeo will die," said Mercutio. "Tybalt is an excellent fighter[1]."

Benvolio knew Mercutio was right, but Romeo was no coward.

If Tybalt challenged him, Romeo would accept, and then Romeo would be killed. Benvolio didn't want to imagine that.

"I'd feel better if we knew where he was," said Benvolio.

"There is our poor lover now," pointed Mercutio.

"Romeo!" cried Benvolio.

"Why did you run away from us last night?" asked Mercutio.

"I'm sorry," said Romeo. "I had something very important to do. What were you so concerned about[2]?"

"About our friend," said Mercutio. "He's been so worried about love lately. We thought he might have done something terrible."

"Have you seen the letter, Romeo?" asked Benvolio.

"Letter?"

"Yes," said Mercutio. "From the house of Capulet, your enemy."

Romeo's eyes lit up[3]. "From the house of Capulet! What did it say?"

---

1. **challenge** [ˈtʃælɪndʒ] (n.) 挑戰
2. **be concerned about** 擔心
3. **light up** 變得明亮 (light-lit-lit)

24

"Why do you sound excited?" asked Benvolio.

"Is it news?" asked Romeo. "I'm so in love. It seems like a thousand years since I last heard her voice. Where is the letter?"

"What do you mean 'her voice'?" asked Benvolio, puzzled[1].

"He's crazy," said Mercutio. "And I must be, too." He rubbed his eyes. "Is that an elephant coming toward us?"

They all looked up and saw Juliet's nurse walking toward them.

"Oh, I see," said Mercutio, loud enough for the nurse to hear. "It's just a fat lady."

"Fat lady!" The nurse turned red with anger and ran toward Mercutio. "You have no manners!"

"Stop this!" yelled Benvolio. "Both of you calm down."

"I was looking for young Romeo here, but I'm sad to see him with such rude men," said the nurse.

"Take him with you," said Mercutio. "A man in love is not good company[2] for bad-mannered[3] men like us."

"What can I do for you, madam?" asked Romeo.

"Can I talk to you in private[4], sir?" asked the nurse.

They stepped aside.

The nurse studied[5] Romeo. "My young lady has told me everything. I have a message from her. But first, she is so young, so do you only pretend to love her?"

"Pretend?" protested[6] Romeo. "I cannot pretend. With Juliet I have discovered myself. My heart, my mind, and my soul belong to her."

The nurse no longer doubted Romeo. She looked into his dark eyes. He was so handsome.

---

1. **puzzled** [ˈpʌzəld] (a.) 困惑的
2. **company** [ˈkʌmpəni] (n.) 同伴
3. **bad-mannered** [bædˈmænərd] (a.) 沒禮貌的
4. **in private** 私下地
5. **study** [ˈstʌdi] (v.) 仔細察看
6. **protest** [prəˈtest] (v.) 抗議

Romeo interrupted her stare[1]. "Are you happy with my answer?"

She blushed[2]. "My lady loves you, and she is very precious[3] to me. What is important to her is important to me. Oh, dear Romeo," she said. "You're going to make Juliet very happy."

Romeo smiled. "I plan to," he said. "I've talked with Friar Lawrence, and he has agreed to marry us. Create a plan, and bring Juliet to the church so we can be married."

"Married," said the nurse. "How beautiful."

"Bring her as soon as you can."

Juliet paced[4] back and forth[5] in her bedroom. She was so impatient.

"I sent her so long ago," she thought. "Why is she so slow?"

She sat down but stood up again. The nurse had been gone for over three hours. How long does it take to walk to the town square?

The door blew open[6], and Juliet heard footsteps[7] coming up the stairs.

"Oh, here she comes!" cried Juliet.

She opened her bedroom door. "Oh, what happened?" she begged. "Did you meet with him? Why do you look so sad?"

1. **stare** [ster] (n.) 凝視
2. **blush** [blʌʃ] (v.) 臉紅
3. **precious** [ˈpreʃəs] (a.) 寶貝的
4. **pace** [peɪs] (v.) 踱步
5. **back and forth** 來來回回
6. **blow open** 吹開
7. **footstep** [ˈfʊtstep] (n.) 腳步聲

Check Up

How does the nurse feel about Romeo's plan to marry Juliet?

a She is jealous of Juliet.

b She thinks Romeo is silly.

c She is excited about it.

Ans: c

26

"Just a minute," said the nurse as she reached the top of the stairs. "I'm out of breath[1]."

Juliet shook her. "Tell me! Is it good news or bad news?"

The nurse pinched her cheek. "You told me his face was more handsome than anyone's, but his hands, his feet, and his whole body are better, too."

The nurse fell onto the bed.

Juliet jumped on top of her. "I know. I know!" she snarled[2]. "But what did he say about our marriage?"

"He said something about it."

"Oh, you tease[3] me!" cried Juliet. "Am I going to be married today or not?"

The nurse grinned[4].

"You didn't want to get married with Paris so quickly. Why are you so eager to[5] marry this Romeo?"

Juliet stood up and straightened herself[6]. "I'm not eager," she said. "But what did Romeo say?"

"Do you have to go to confession[7] today?"

"Stop teasing me! Tell me what Romeo said!"

Juliet was frustrated[8] and fell onto the bed.

The nurse felt sorry for her. "Okay, okay, I was only teasing you. A young woman that is going to get married can forgive me." She smiled.

"Married?" The word echoed[9] in Juliet's head.

"Now if you want to make any confessions, you have to go to church. There you will find a young man who is eager to marry you." She smiled again.

Juliet gasped.

Juliet hugged[10] the nurse. "Thank you! Thank you!" she cried. "Let's go right now!"

1. **out of breath** 喘不過氣來
2. **snarl** [snɑːrl] (v.) 咆哮
3. **tease** [tiːz] (v.) 取笑
4. **grin** [grɪn] (v.) 露齒而笑 (grin-grinned-grinned)
5. **eager to** 渴望；急切
6. **straighten oneself** 直起身子
7. **confession** [kən'feʃən] (n.) 告解
8. **frustrated** ['frʌstreɪtid] (a.) 洩氣的
9. **echo** ['ekoʊ] (v.) 回響
10. **hug** [hʌg] (v.) 擁抱 (hug-hugged-hugged)

Short answer question.

What excuse will Juliet make to her family for going to church?

Ans: She is going to church to make confessions.

Friar Lawrence was preparing Romeo for the wedding. He wasn't sure if this wedding was the right thing to do. Marrying two young people without their parents' permission[1] was not right. He wanted this marriage to bring the two families closer together, but he wasn't sure if it would.

"Will they get angry? Will they get angry with me?" he thought.

"Amen already," said Romeo. He was impatient from waiting on[2] Friar Lawrence.

"Calm yourself, Romeo," scolded Friar Lawrence. "You need to live and love moderately[3]. If not, neither love nor life will last[4] long."

But he knew Romeo wouldn't be calm. Neither would Juliet. Then Juliet came running toward the church.

"I should send both of them home," thought Friar Lawrence. But he knew he couldn't do that.

"Good afternoon, Father," sang Juliet. She jumped into Romeo's arms.

"Juliet!" cried Romeo, holding her. "Please tell me you love me as much as I love you! And how happy you will be after we are married."

"I love you so much that words can't describe it," she said and kissed him.

"Okay, enough," said Friar Lawrence, separating[5] the two. "Let's hurry with the wedding."

---

1. **permission** [pərˈmɪʃən] (n.) 允許
2. **wait on** 等候
3. **moderately** [ˈmɑːdərɪtli] (adv.) 節制地；適度地
4. **last** [læst] (v.) 持續
5. **separate** [ˈsepəret] (v.) 使分離

Check Up

Why did Friar Lawrence have doubts about the wedding?

a He thinks Romeo and Juliet would stop loving each other soon.

b He thinks Lords Capulet and Montague might be angry with him.

c He thinks Romeo is not sincere.

Ans: b

Friar Lawrence took them to the altar[1]. Then he quickly performed[2] the wedding ceremony[3]. When he was through[4], he left them to pray, and he went to the garden to think.

The nurse found him there. "Romeo isn't welcome in Juliet's house," she said. "Nor she in his. What are they going to do?"

"I haven't thought about that," replied Friar Lawrence. "Maybe they can tell their parents soon."

"Father," the nurse smiled. "They are newlyweds[5]. They want to be together."

"You are like a mother to Juliet. You should have thought about this problem before the wedding," snapped Friar Lawrence.

"You married them," she replied. "You should have thought about this problem, too."

"They need our help, so how can we solve this problem?" asked Friar Lawrence.

"Their parents will kill us if they find out about this. We have to keep it a secret[6] for a while. But we have to give these two time to be man and wife together. I'm sure they'll be okay after a while."

"Right," agreed Friar Lawrence. "Take Juliet home. I'll help Romeo find a way to go into her bedroom tonight. That should solve the problem for a while. We'll worry about the parents later."

---

1. **altar** [ˈɑːltər] (n.) 教堂聖壇
2. **perform** [pərˈfɔːrm] (v.) 執行
3. **ceremony** [ˈserəməni] (n.) 儀式
4. **be through** 完成
5. **newlyweds** [ˈnjuːliwedz] (n.) 新婚夫妻
6. **keep A secret** 保密

Understanding the Story

Love, Hate and Fate in "Romeo and Juliet"

Shakespeare explores many themes in his play "Romeo and Juliet". The most important of these themes are love, hate and fate.

Shakespeare shows his audience[1] many kinds of love. One type of love in this play is "infatuation[2]". Sometimes this love is called "puppy love[3]".

Many teenagers fall into this type of love. They don't realize that their feelings are actually an obsession[4], not true love. Romeo's love for Rosaline is an example of this type of love. Most importantly, we can see true love in this play. This love is so strong that Romeo and Juliet will even sacrifice[5] their lives for it.

Shakespeare also has an important lesson for his audience about hate. Hate always leads to tragedy[6], as in the needless[7] deaths of "Romeo and Juliet." Too late, the Capulets and the Montagues learn this lesson through the deaths of their children.

Finally, Shakespeare addresses[8] the idea of fate. At the beginning of the play, the author mentions that Romeo and Juliet are "star-crossed[9]" lovers. This means that whatever they do, they cannot escape their destiny. They are doomed to never be happy together. Romeo and Juliet struggle[10] against their fate, and do bold[11] things to try to be together. But in the end, they cannot overcome[12] the fate that has already been decided for them.

1. **audience** ['ɔːdiəns] (n.) 觀眾
2. **infatuation** [ɪnˌfætʃu'eɪʃən] (n.) 著迷；熱戀
3. **puppy love** 純純的愛
4. **obsession** [əb'seʃən] (n) 迷戀
5. **sacrifice** ['sækrɪfaɪs] (v.) 犧牲
6. **tragedy** ['trædʒədi] (n.) 悲劇
7. **needless** ['niːdləs] (a.) 不必要的
8. **address** [ə'dres] (v.) 強調
9. **star-crossed** ['stɑːrˌkrɒːsd] (a.) 不幸的
10. **struggle** ['strʌgəl] (v.) 對抗
11. **bold** [boʊld] (a.) 大膽的
12. **overcome** [ˌoʊvər'kʌm] (v.) 克服

Chapter Four

29

The Swordfight in the Square

A messenger[1] came and gave Benvolio some news. It was the Capulets. They were looking for Romeo.

"Tybalt is really angry," Benvolio said to Mercutio. "I think we should get out of[2] here."

"I won't go," said Mercutio.

"I don't want to be here when they come," insisted[3] Benvolio. "I don't want to get into[4] a fight."

Just then, Benvolio saw Tybalt and some of his friends making their way[5] across the street.

"Oh, no!" said Benvolio. "Here come the Capulets. Let's go!"

"I'm not worried about them," replied Mercutio.

It was too late to leave.

"Good afternoon," said Tybalt. "Can I speak with one of you?"

"Speak with us?" said Mercutio. "That's a strange way to ask someone to fight."

"I will fight if you give me a reason," answered Tybalt, putting a hand on his sword. He stepped closer. "Mercutio, Romeo was with you last night, right? Where is he now?"

"Do I look like a slave?" asked Mercutio. "Am I supposed to answer your every question? Even if I did know where Romeo was, I wouldn't tell you."

Tybalt drew his sword.

"Gentlemen," interrupted Benvolio. "Either stop this fight, or go somewhere else to finish it. Everyone is watching us."

---

1. **messenger** [ˈmesɪndʒər] (n.) 信差
2. **get out of** 離開
3. **insist** [ɪnˈsɪst] (v.) 堅持
4. **get into** 陷入
5. **make one's way** 朝某個方向走去

"No need," said Tybalt. He saw Romeo walking toward them. "Here comes my man."

"Your man?" said Mercutio, teasing Tybalt. "Is he one of your servants?"

"A mistake," said Tybalt, as Romeo came up to[1] them.

"I should have called him a villain[2] instead!" He looked at Romeo.

Romeo just smiled. "Tybalt," he said, "I love you, so I will forgive your anger. You will soon learn that I'm not a villain. Until then, goodbye."

Tybalt thought Romeo was just making fun of him. "You ruined[3] our party last night with your presence. Now turn, and draw your sword!" shouted Tybalt.

"I've never hurt you, Tybalt. And I couldn't now. I love you like a brother. More like a brother than you know." He bowed. "Be happy."

Mercutio looked at Romeo. "He's being dishonorable[4]! Why is he acting like this?"

"I think he's being reasonable," said Benvolio. "Let's peacefully go away and be happy."

"I'll be happy when Tybalt is dead!" said Mercutio.

Tybalt lifted his sword. "I'm ready for you!"

"Tybalt! Mercutio!" said Romeo. "Put your swords away!"

Mercutio pushed Romeo aside and lunged at Tybalt. Tybalt stepped aside. Then he began swinging[5] his sword at Mercutio.

"Tybalt! Mercutio! The prince has forbidden[6] this! Stop!" Romeo shouted. "Benvolio, help me stop this fight."

Romeo stepped between the two and grabbed Mercutio. But Tybalt kept coming. Mercutio tried to defend himself, but Romeo was holding him too tightly. Tybalt's sword stuck[7] into Mercutio's chest[8].

---

1. **come up to** 走向
2. **villain** [ˈvɪlən] (n.) 壞人；惡棍
3. **ruin** [ˈruːɪn] (v.) 破壞
4. **dishonorable** [dɪsˈɑːnərəbəl] (a.) 丟臉的
5. **swing** [swɪŋ] (v.) 揮舞 (swing-swung-swung)
6. **forbid** [fərˈbɪd] (v.) 禁止 (forbid-forbade-forbidden)
7. **stick** [stɪk] (v.) 刺；插
8. **chest** [tʃest] (n.) 胸部

Check Up

Romeo told Tybalt ________________.

a that Romeo loved him like a brother

b that Tybalt had better go home before he got killed

c that Tybalt was a coward

Ans: a

31

"Ahhhh!" Mercutio cried, falling to the ground.

Tybalt withdrew[1] his sword and wiped off[2] the blood.

Benvolio ran to Mercutio. "How bad is it?"

"It's enough." Mercutio coughed. He put his hand over his chest. Blood gushed[3] through his fingers.

"Be brave," said Romeo. "You'll be okay."

"No," said Mercutio, his senses[4] leaving him. "I won't be okay."

Blood began to come out of his mouth. "Why did you come between us, Romeo? I couldn't defend myself."

Romeo looked into his friend's eyes. "I was trying to stop you."

"You stopped me, all right." Mercutio gasped. "He has killed me."

"I'll take him to the doctor," said Benvolio. As he prepared to lift him, he felt his pulse[5] fade away[6]. "He's dead," he said.

Romeo stared at Mercutio. "My friend was killed because of me," he thought. "And Tybalt teases us all. Oh, Juliet, I wish I could have married you one day later. Then Tybalt would not be my cousin, and I could take revenge[7] on him."

Romeo became so angry that the love and tenderness[8] that he had felt began to disappear. In a second[9], he forgot about Juliet, about his marriage, and about the future. He wanted justice[10]. He wanted revenge.

He picked up Mercutio's sword.

"Romeo," said Benvolio, "put the sword away. Here comes Tybalt."

Romeo didn't put the sword down. "So you've returned to see Mercutio's dead body. And to see us cry at your feet. No. No, Tybalt!" he yelled.

---

1. **withdraw** [wɪð'drɔ:] (v.) 抽回 (withdraw-withdrew-withdrawn)
2. **wipe off** 擦掉
3. **gush** [gʌʃ] (v.) 噴；湧
4. **sense** [sens] (n.) 意識
5. **pulse** [pʌls] (n.) 脈搏
6. **fade away** 逐漸消失（微弱）
7. **revenge** [rɪ'vendʒ] (n.) 報仇
8. **tenderness** ['tendərnəs] (n.) 溫柔
9. **in a second** 瞬間
10. **justice** ['dʒʌstɪs] (n.) 正義

32

Tybalt strutted[1] up to Romeo. "You poor little boy," he said. "Do you want to die just like Mercutio?"

"My sword is strong!" Romeo said, and he struck[2] at Tybalt.

Tybalt blocked Romeo's blow[3] with ease. But Romeo pressed on[5] with incredible[6] speed. Tybalt tried to keep calm. He tried to make it appear as if he could easily defend against Romeo's attacks. It soon became clear that he was not fighting a man, but an avenging[7] angel.

Romeo swung at Tybalt so violently[8] that he could no longer feel his arm or the sword. He kept raging[9] forward. As he did, he saw Tybalt's eyes change from being confident[10] to panic[11] and then to horror[12].

Suddenly, there was no more ringing[13] of swords. No more shouting. The vicious[14] face of Tybalt became peaceful. It was then that Romeo saw how much he looked like Juliet. He watched Tybalt fall to the ground.

"Let's get out of here!" yelled Benvolio. "Tybalt's dead. The prince will kill you all if he finds you here."

Romeo dropped his sword. It was covered with Tybalt's blood. The blood of Juliet's kinsman.

"Oh, I'm a fool," he said.

"They are coming!" Benvolio screamed[15]. "Romeo, get out of here!"

---

1. **strut** [strʌt] (v.) 趾高氣揚地走
2. **strike** [straɪk] (v.) 攻擊 (strike-struck-struck)
3. **blow** [bloʊ] (n.) 用拳或武器等的一擊
4. **press on** 奮力前進
5. **incredible** [ɪn'kredɪbəl] (a.) 驚人的
6. **avenging** [ə'vendʒɪŋ] (a.) 復仇的
7. **violently** ['vaɪələntli] (adv.) 猛烈狂暴地
8. **rage** [reɪdʒ] (v.) 激烈進行
9. **confident** ['kɑːnfɪdənt] (a.) 自信的
10. **panic** ['pænɪk] (n.) 驚恐
11. **vicious** ['vɪʃəs] (a.) 兇惡的

Check Up

Why must Romeo run away?

a The prince will kill him if he sees him there.

b Tybalt will surely kill Romeo.

c They must get Mercutio to a doctor.

33

Juliet stood on her balcony. She watched the sunset.

"Please leave us, sun," she chanted[1]. "Quickly become dark so that Romeo can come into my bedroom. Then we can hold each other all night."

The nurse slipped[2] through the curtain and out onto the balcony. She looked worried.

Juliet knew something was wrong. "What's the matter?"

"He's dead," she said.

Juliet almost fainted[3]. "My Romeo? My love? Dead?"

"No," said the nurse, but the truth wasn't much better. "No. Tybalt. Tybalt is dead. Killed by Romeo. And Romeo has been banished[4] by the prince."

"Did Romeo really kill Tybalt?" Juliet could barely speak as she started to cry.

"There are no honest men," replied the nurse. "I hope something bad happens to Romeo."

Juliet became angry. "Don't say that!"

"He killed your cousin. How can you defend him?"

"Should I hate my husband? My cousin would have killed Romeo. But my husband is still alive." Juliet tried to stop crying. "So why can't I stop crying? I should be glad that Romeo is still alive."

The tears came again. "Banished! He will never come to Verona or me again."

1. **chant** [tʃænt] (v.) 吟誦
2. **slip** [slɪp] (v.) 悄悄走
3. **faint** [feɪnt] (v.) 昏倒
4. **banish** [ˈbænɪʃ] (v.) 流放

One Point Lesson

I hope **something bad** happens to Romeo.
我希望厄運降臨在羅密歐的身上。

something + adj.：表示……樣的事。當不定代名詞 something、anything、nothing 出現時，形容詞置於其後做為修飾

e.g. Would you like **something cold**? 你要來點冰的東西嗎？

Romeo stood up when Friar Lawrence returned to his room. "Well, Father? What news? What did the prince decide?"

Friar Lawrence removed his jacket and hung it on the coat rack[1]. "A gentle judgment," he said, knowing that Romeo would not agree. "Not death, but banishment."

"Banishment!" Romeo cried. "Banishment is worse than death! Please say 'death'."

Friar Lawrence knew Romeo was saying this because of his love for Juliet. "The prince could have killed you. He didn't. The prince is being kind."

There was a loud knock on the door.

"Hide yourself, Romeo," said Friar Lawrence.

Romeo hid as Friar Lawrence opened the door. It was the nurse.

"Good afternoon, Friar," she said. "Is Romeo here?"

"He is very sad, but here," he said. "Romeo!"

He came forward.

"He looks like Juliet," said the nurse. "Tears and crying."

"You break my heart[2], nurse," said Romeo, "to speak of Juliet."

"And you broke her heart," she said. "She wants to see Tybalt and you, but she can't see either."

"Because I'm the bad guy that murdered[3] her cousin," said Romeo. "I will make Juliet happy and kill that bad guy."

He pulled out his knife and placed[4] it against his chest.

1. **rack** [ræk] (n.) 掛物架
2. **break one's heart** 讓……心碎
3. **murder** [ˈmɜːrdər] (v.) 謀殺
4. **place** [pleɪs] (v.) 放置

35

"Don't do that!" Friar Lawrence knocked the knife out of Romeo's hands.

"You amaze[1] me. You killed Tybalt by mistake. But if you kill yourself, you will also be killing Juliet. She is still alive. Will you abandon[2] her by killing[3] yourself? The prince has given you life. Calm down, and think about what you will do."

Romeo collapsed[4] in a chair. Friar Lawrence put his hand on Romeo's head. "Meet your love tonight. Go to her room as we have planned. Comfort[5] her. We will get you out of the city after you have done this. You can live in Mantua until we can fix[6] things between your families. If your love is strong enough, it will endure."

"Good idea," said the nurse. "I'll go and tell Juliet you will come tonight."

---

1. **amaze** [ə'meɪz] (v.) 使驚愕
2. **abandon** [ə'bændən] (v.) 背棄
3. **by V-ing** 藉由……方式
4. **collapse** [kə'læps] (v.) 虛脫
5. **comfort** ['kʌmfərt] (v.) 安慰
6. **fix** [fɪks] (v.) 修復
7. **make a mistake** 犯錯

Capulet was at his home with Paris. Because of Tybalt's death, he realized that many of the young people didn't listen to him. Tybalt hadn't listened to him, and so he had died. Capulet didn't want his only daughter to make the same mistake[7].

"Wife," he commanded, "speak to Juliet before you go to bed. Tell her that Paris loves her. Tell her that on Thursday, three days from now, she will marry Paris."

Lady Capulet bowed and left.

"Is this okay with you?" Capulet asked Paris.

"Of course. I only wish that we could marry tomorrow," he answered.

A Fill in the blanks with the given words.

prune scold eager confession altar

1. Juliet couldn't wait. She was ___________ to marry Romeo.
2. Romeo and Juliet were married at the ___________.
3. Friar Lawrence ___________ Romeo for falling in love with Rosaline.
4. Friar Lawrence was in the garden ___________ the flowers.
5. At ___________, Juliet would tell her sins to Friar Lawrence.

B Rearrange the sentences in chronological order.

1. Romeo was banished from Verona.
2. Tybalt was looking for Romeo.
3. Romeo killed Tybalt.
4. Tybalt spoke with Mercutio.
5. Tybalt and Mercutio started fighting.

_____ ⇨ _____ ⇨ _____ ⇨ _____ ⇨ _____

C Choose the correct answer.

1. Why did Friar Lawrence agree to marry Romeo and Juliet?
   (a) Romeo and Juliet were in love.
   (b) He thought the marriage would bring peace to the two families.
   (c) The prince wanted Friar Lawrence to marry them.

2. Why did the nurse visit Romeo?
   (a) To find out about the wedding.
   (b) To tell him Juliet loved him.
   (c) To convince Romeo not to marry Juliet.

3. Why did Romeo fight with Tybalt?
   (a) Because Tybalt wanted to fight.
   (b) Because Tybalt killed Mercutio.
   (c) Because Tybalt found out about the secret wedding.

4. What did Romeo think about the judgment?
   (a) The prince was kind.
   (b) Banishment was worse than death.
   (c) Punishment was very light.

Chapter Five

36 The Secret Plan

Upstairs[1] in Juliet's bedroom, Romeo kissed his lover's lips.

"Why do you have to leave so soon?" Juliet asked.

"I must go and live or stay and die."

"Stay, and we will die together," she said as she hugged[2] him.

He kissed her again. "I will if you will."

"My lady!" whispered the nurse as she opened the bedroom door. "Your mother is coming."

"Goodbye, my wife, my love," said Romeo. "One more kiss, and I'll leave."

He moved her hair and kissed her forehead[3].

"My husband," said Juliet. "I must hear from you every day."

"Goodbye," he said again. "I'll write you every day."

"When will we meet again?"

"Soon . . ."

"Hurry!" cried the nurse.

"I'm frightened," said Juliet.

"Trust me," Romeo said.

He kissed her and climbed down the balcony.

"How are you, Juliet?" Lady Capulet asked, opening the door.

"I'm not well," said Juliet, dressing[4] quickly.

"Still crying over[5] your cousin's death?" Lady Capulet asked. "We are all upset[6]."

---

1. **upstairs** [ʌp'sterz] (adv.) 樓上
2. **hug** [hʌg] (v.) 擁抱 (hug-hugged-hugged)
3. **forehead** ['fɔːrhed] (n.) 前額
4. **dress** [dres] (v.) 穿衣
5. **cry over** 為……而哭
6. **upset** [ʌp'set] (a.) 難過的

37

Her mother then gave her the news. "Next Thursday morning, you will marry Paris at Saint[1] Peter's Church."

"No, I will not!" Juliet yelled before she had time to think about what she was saying.

Lady Capulet was angry. "You disobey[2] ?"

"I mean," Juliet said, "it is impossible."

Footsteps were coming up the stairs outside the bedroom. "Your father is coming. Tell him yourself."

Capulet came into the bedroom.

"Father," Juliet said, "I cannot marry Paris."

"But I desire[3] you to marry him," Capulet said.

"I understand, but I cannot."

"Do my desires mean nothing to you?"

"They are very important to me, but I'm unable to[4] marry Paris."

"How can you disobey me?" yelled Capulet. "Am I the master of this house? You will marry Paris next Thursday!"

1. **Saint** [seɪnt] (n.) 聖（縮寫為 St，用於教堂等專有名詞前）
2. **disobey** [dɪsə'beɪ] (v.) 違背
3. **desire** [dɪ'zaɪr] (v.) 渴望
4. **unable to** 無法

“Please father!” cried Juliet, falling and grabbing her father’s ankles. “You’ve always let me make my own decisions. Please, let me make my own decision now.”

“Decisions? I’ll give you a decision to make. Marry Paris next Thursday, or never look at me again. Don’t speak! Just do it!” he said.

Juliet cried and held her mother. Lady Capulet pushed her away. “Your father is only doing what’s best for you. Don’t speak anymore.” She left Juliet alone with the nurse.

"How can we prevent[1] this? Say something! What can I do?"

The nurse didn't have an answer. She knew if Juliet was gone, she would have no job and wouldn't be able to support herself.

"Nurse?" pleaded[2] Juliet.

"All right," she said, "here is my advice[3]. Romeo's banished and can never come back. He's the only one that knows you're married. Well, I know, and Friar Lawrence knows, but we won't say a word. Do you understand? If you marry Paris, only Romeo can challenge[4] the marriage. But he won't because he will never come back to Verona."

Juliet was shocked. "Are you serious?" She looked into the nurse's eyes.

"It's the only way," she said. "Paris will make a lovely husband!"

"Thank you, nurse," said Juliet stiffly. "You don't have to say anything else. Go tell my mother and father that I will marry Paris."

The nurse felt sick to her stomach as she watched Juliet go to the door and hold it open. The girl was like her own daughter. Juliet had come to her for help, and all she could do was lie. What was worse, Juliet knew that she had lied.

"I said I will do it, nurse," said Juliet, crossing her arms[5]. "So you may go. I will go to Friar Lawrence in the morning and confess[6] my sins[7]."

1. **prevent** [prɪˈvent] (v.) 防止
2. **plead** [pliːd] (v.) 懇求
3. **advice** [ədˈvaɪs] (n.) 忠告
4. **challenge** [ˈtʃælɪndʒ] (v.) 提出質疑或異議
5. **cross one's arms** 手臂交叉
6. **confess** [kənˈfes] (v.) 告解
7. **sin** [sɪn] (n.) 罪孽

Meanwhile[1], Paris was at the church talking to Friar Lawrence.

"Thursday is too soon," said the friar.

"That's what her father wants," said Paris.

"But what does Juliet say?"

"She is too upset because of her cousin's death," Paris explained. "But her father says she will marry me."

"I'm sorry," said Friar Lawrence, "but you are hurrying this wedding, and you don't even know what Juliet thinks. I don't like it."

"Friar Lawrence!" came a voice.

Friar Lawrence looked down the path and saw Juliet running through the garden.

"Oh, someday she will call my name and run to me like that," said Paris.

Friar Lawrence ignored[2] him. "What is it?"

She froze when she saw Paris. "Nothing, Father," she said. "I have come to make confession."

"Hello, Juliet." Paris bowed.

Juliet bowed and looked at Friar Lawrence for help.

"Paris," he said, "you must give us time alone."

"Of course," he said. "Juliet, I will see you on Thursday."

He waved goodbye and walked away.

"Oh, Juliet," said Friar Lawrence. "I hear you must marry Paris on Thursday."

Juliet looked at him. "Certainly, Friar, you will prevent this from happening[3]."

Friar Lawrence looked at Juliet.

"Please understand . . ."

1. **meanwhile** [ˈmiːnwaɪl] (adv.) 同時
2. **ignore** [ɪgˈnɔːr] (v.) 忽視
3. **prevent *A* from V-ing** 防止A免於……

"I see how it is," said Juliet. "First my nurse and now you. You married Romeo and me. But now you won't prevent this second, unlawful[1] marriage."

She angrily walked away but stopped short[2] and turned. "You amaze me, you older people. You are so brave when there is nothing to fear, but when there is trouble, you run away. Is this the wisdom[3] of older people? Well, I was prepared for this!" She pulled out a knife.

"Juliet!" exclaimed[4] Friar Lawrence, "what are you doing?"

She put the knife against her heart. "Since you will not help, this knife will solve our problem."

"Wait!" cried Friar Lawrence. "There is another way."

"How?"

Friar Lawrence thought quickly. "Here," he said, pulling some flowers from his garden.

"I will make a potion[5] from these flowers. The drink will cause[6] a death-like[7] sleep. When you are at home alone in your bedroom, drink this potion. You will feel cold and sleepy, even your pulse will stop. Later, when your family takes your body to your family tomb[8], I will come and get you. I'll tell Romeo of this plan by letter. He will come too! Don't be afraid."

A determined[9] look came over[10] Juliet's face. "Give it to me! I'm not afraid."

Friar Lawrence went into his kitchen and prepared the potion.

1. **unlawful** [ʌn'lɔːfəl] (a.) 不合法的
2. **stop short** 突然停止
3. **wisdom** ['wɪzdəm] (n.) 智慧
4. **exclaim** [ɪk'skleɪm] (v.) 大聲叫
5. **potion** ['poʊʃən] (n.) 藥劑
6. **cause** [kɔːz] (v.) 造成
7. **death-like** ['deθˌlaɪk] (a.) 死了一樣的
8. **tomb** [tuːm] (n.) 墳墓
9. **determined** [dɪ'tɜːrmɪnd] (a.) 下定決心的
10. **come over** (某感覺) 影響……

Check Up

What will the friar do for Juliet?

a He will help her commit suicide.
b He will tell Romeo to come rescue Juliet.
c He will make a potion for Juliet.

Ans: c

The nurse put Juliet's wedding dress on her bed. "You'll be a beautiful bride[1]," she said. "Paris is a lucky man."

Capulet and his wife stood on the side.

Juliet looked at them. "I'm happy to have a great father and mother."

She gave a half smile and bowed.

"You are a perfect lady," said Capulet.

Juliet moved the wedding dress and sat down.

"Please excuse[2] me, and leave me alone for the night. I must pray."

"Let's go. Leave her to pray," said Capulet. "Daughter, you have made me very happy."

He hobbled[3] out of the bedroom.

"Should I wait beside you tonight?" the nurse asked.

"Thank you," Juliet didn't even look at the nurse, "but that's okay. You've done enough for me already."

The words hurt the nurse's feelings.

"I would do anything for you. You know that," the nurse said softly[4].

"Then leave me," Juliet said.

The nurse walked out of the room.

"Get some sleep," said Lady Capulet. "You will need it." She left.

1. **bride** [braɪd] (n.) 新娘
2. **excuse** [ɪk'skjuːz] (v.) 原諒
3. **hobble** ['hɑːbəl] (v.) 跛行
4. **softly** [sɒːftli] (adv.) 輕聲地

Juliet silently closed the door and took out the potion Friar Lawrence had given her. She held it tightly. She had a thought. What if she woke up before Romeo came? Wouldn't she suffocate[1] in the family tomb? Worse, what if, surrounded[2] by horrible[3] images[4] of death, she became crazy? What if, waking up beside Tybalt, she became mad? What if . . .

"Enough of 'what ifs,'" she whispered. "This is the only answer."

She put the bottle to her lips. "Romeo, I drink this for you." She drank.

Her throat burned. She gagged[5]. Bright lights appeared before her. Her body went numb[6]. She felt herself falling. And then nothing.

1. **suffocate** [ˈsʌfəkeɪt] (v.) 窒息
2. **surround** [səˈraʊnd] (v.) 圍繞
3. **horrible** [ˈhɔːrɪbəl] (a.) 恐怖的
4. **image** [ˈɪmɪdʒ] (n.) 影像
5. **gag** [ɡæɡ] (v.) 窒息 (gag-gagged-gagged)
6. **numb** [nʌm] (a.) 麻木的
7. **encouragement** [ɪnˈkɜːrɪdʒmənt] (n.) 鼓勵

Before dawn, the nurse woke up and went to Juliet's room. "One word of encouragement[7]," she mumbled. "That's all. Surely Juliet will listen to me."

She opened Juliet's door and tiptoed to where the young lady was sleeping. She put her hand on her cold forehead. Her scream woke up the entire house.

Check Up

Choose all the things that Juliet worries about.

a She worries about waking up too soon.

b She worries that the potion will really kill her.

c She worries about seeing Tybalt's dead body.

Understanding the Story

"Romeo and Juliet" Forever

William Shakespeare's plays are very famous even today because the themes[1] about which he writes are universal[2]. His characters experience human emotions and situations that are similar in any culture, at any time. This is why Shakespeare's plays can be so easily changed to different settings[3] in modern movies and plays.

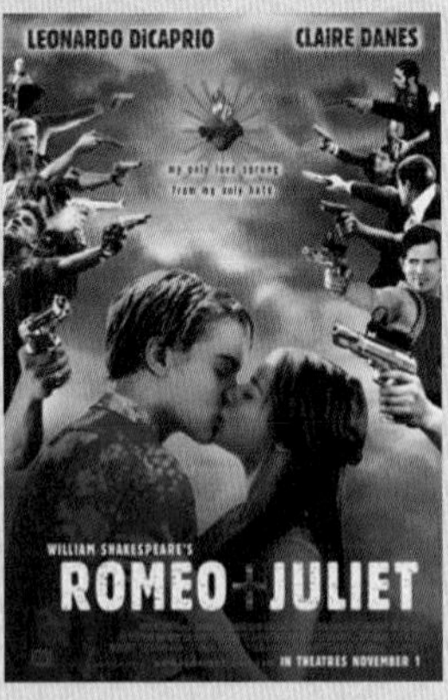

Romeo and Juliet is probably Shakespeare's most adaptable[4] work. Theater companies all over the world stage[5] many different versions of this play. Movie directors have also adapted this story for unique productions[6].

One of the most well known of these movies was the 1996 movie *Romeo + Juliet* starring[7] Leonardo DiCaprio and Claire Danes. This movie was set in modern times, with the youthful[8] Capulets and Montagues fighting their battles[9] with handguns instead of swords.

Sometimes, the movie versions don't even mention the name "Romeo and Juliet", but just borrow the basic plot[10]. This is the case with the 1961 film *West Side Story* which was instantly popular and is still popular today.

In this version, Romeo is Tony, and Juliet is Maria. The scene is the Upper West Side of New York, a tough neighborhood that saw frequent violence between street gangs[11] in the 60's. Tony and Maria are associated with rival gangs. However, in this version, Maria does not die. After Tony is shot by a rival[12] gang member, Maria manages to bring peace between the gangs.

In these versions and many others, the universal themes of Shakespeare continue to live on.

1. **theme** [θiːm] (n.) 主題
2. **universal** [ˌjuːnɪˈvɜːrsəl] (a.) 普遍的
3. **setting** [ˈsetɪŋ] (n.) 場景
4. **adaptable** [əˈdæptəbəl] (a.) 可改編的
5. **stage** [steɪdʒ] (v.) 演出
6. **production** [prəˈdʌkʃən] (n.) 作品
7. **star** [stɑːr] (v.) 主演
8. **youthful** [ˈjuːθfəl] (a.) 年輕的
9. **battle** [ˈbætl] (n.) 戰鬥
10. **plot** [plɑːt] (n.) 情節
11. **gang** [gæŋ] (n.) 幫派
12. **rival** [ˈraɪvəl] (a.) 敵對的

Chapter Six

The Lovers' Tragedy

Balthasar's hand shook as he opened the door of Romeo's apartment in Mantua.

"Ah," Romeo said, "news from Verona? Do you have a letter from the friar? How's my father? How's my Juliet?"

"Her soul is with the angels," answered Balthasar.

"Her soul is always with the angels," Romeo smiled, "but what about the rest of her?"

"Her body is in the Capulet's tomb."

Romeo rose from his desk. "What do you mean?"

"I . . . saw her body in the tomb. She . . . she is dead."

"That can't be[1] true!"

"I wish it weren't true."

"Go, Balthasar. Get me a horse. Meet me by the city walls. I will leave tonight."

"Please, don't go, sir," said Balthasar, "You are angry, and nothing good will happen because of this."

Romeo gathered his things and packed them into a bag. "You are mistaken. This is not anger. It is a reasonable[2] response[3] to these events. Now go, and do what I told you!"

Balthasar left.

"Juliet," said Romeo, "I will lie with you tonight."

But how, he wondered. Then he remembered. There was a man in Mantua who sold strange drugs. He threw his bag over his shoulder and walked out.

As soon as he walked out, a monk[4] arrived at Romeo's apartment.

"Hello!" he cried. "I have a letter for Romeo! Hello? It comes from Friar Lawrence, and it's very important! Is anyone there? Hello?"

No one was there to answer.

---

1. **can't (cannot) be** 不可能是……
2. **reasonable** [ˈriːzənəbəl] (a.) 合理的
3. **response** [rɪˈspɑːns] (n.) 回應
4. **monk** [mʌŋk] (n.) 修道士

44 Friar Lawrence stayed hidden as he walked to the Capulet's family tomb. By looking at the moon, he could tell that it was almost midnight[1]. That meant that Juliet would wake up soon. He didn't want to think about Juliet waking up in a cold tomb surrounded by[2] dead bones.

He walked faster until he arrived at the crossroads[3] where he had instructed[4] Romeo to meet him.

There was nobody there.

He waited for a long time, but there was no Romeo. Finally, he saw a man walking toward him, but it didn't look like Romeo.

"Who else would be coming to the graveyard at this time of night?" he thought.

"Who's there?" called Friar Lawrence.

"Friar Lawrence?" returned the voice. "Is that you?"

"Friar John?" asked Friar Lawrence, squinting[5] to see who it was.

"Yes," said Friar John.

"What are you doing here?" asked Friar Lawrence. "Where is Romeo?"

"That's what I came to talk to you about."

"Did you take the letter to Romeo?"

"I never got the chance to," said Friar John. "I was stuck[6] at the customs[7] house. By the time I got to Mantua, Romeo was gone."

"Oh, no," said Friar Lawrence. "I'm sure he has heard about Juliet's death by now and has . . . has . . . dear God, what has he done?"

"You seem upset, my brother."

"Go to my house," Friar Lawrence said. "Wait there in case Romeo shows up. Tell him Juliet is alive."

Friar John didn't really understand, but he did as he was told.

1. **midnight** [ˈmɪdnaɪt] (n.) 午夜
2. **surrounded by** 被……圍繞
3. **crossroads** [ˈkrɒːsroʊdz] (n.) 十字路
4. **instruct** [ɪnˈstrʌkt] (v.) 指示
5. **squint** [skwɪnt] (v.) 瞇著眼看
6. **stuck** [stʌk] (a.) 被困住的
7. **customs** [ˈkʌstəms] (n.) 海關

45

"Wait here with the torch[1]," said Paris to his servant.

The servant went to the side of the road while Paris went to the Capulet's tomb. He dropped flowers in front of the tomb. "This," he told himself, "I will do this every night to show how much I loved Juliet."

As he dropped the flowers, he heard his servant whistle. Was it a ghost? Paris looked across the graveyard[2] and saw a man approaching. He hid himself behind a large tombstone.

"It was no ghost," thought Paris. "It was Romeo! With a crowbar[3]! The man who killed Tybalt. Now he has come to destroy[4] the tomb! Not while I'm here!"

Romeo started to open the door with the crowbar.

"Stop right there, villain," Paris commanded, stepping forward.

"Don't try to stop me," Romeo said without looking up. "Leave me alone!"

The door groaned[5] open. Paris grabbed Romeo by the arm.

1. **torch** [tɔːrtʃ] (n.) 火把
2. **graveyard** [ˈɡreɪvjɑːrd] (n.) 墓園
3. **crowbar** [ˈkroʊbɑːr] (n.) 鐵撬
4. **destroy** [dɪˈstrɔɪ] (v.) 破壞

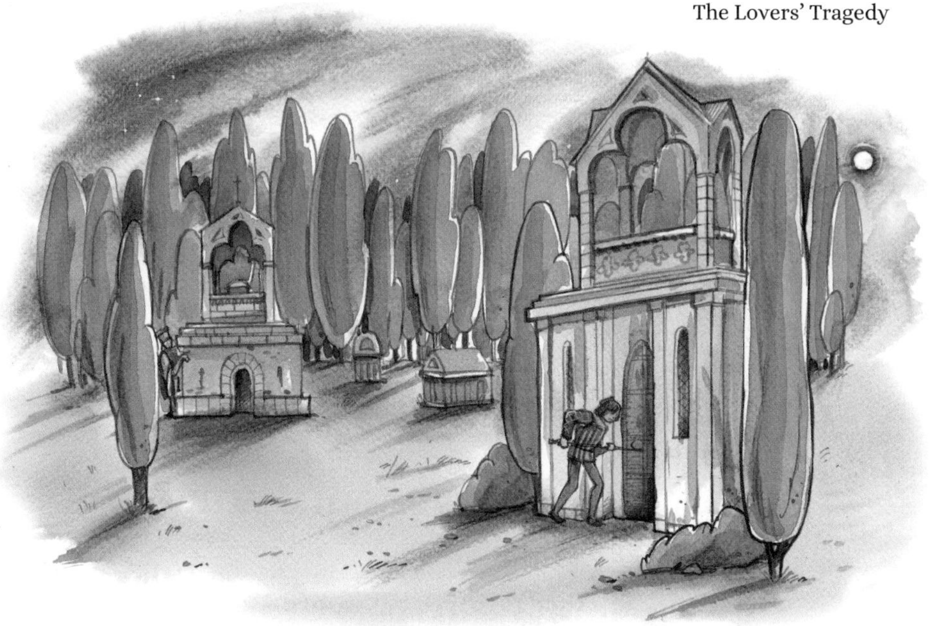

When Romeo felt his hand, he spun around and swung[6] the crowbar, hitting Paris in the head. Paris fell dead[7] to the ground. His servant, who had been watching, ran off[8] to tell the soldiers.

5. **groan** [groʊn] (v.) 發嘎吱聲
6. **swing** [swɪŋ] (v.) 揮舞
7. **fall dead** 死掉
8. **run off** 跑掉（走）

Check Up

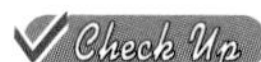

Why was Paris at Juliet's tomb?

a He wanted to say a final farewell to his love.
b He heard Romeo would try to ruin the tomb.
c He wanted to show his love for Juliet.

Ans: c

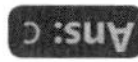

46

Romeo dragged Paris' body into the tomb. There on a stone he found Juliet's body.

Romeo fell to his knees[1]. "Oh, my love, my wife," he said, "you are still so beautiful, even in death."

He brushed the hair back from Juliet's face.

"You are the last thing I want to see on this earth."

He pressed his lips against hers. Then he opened a small bottle.

"Here is to my love!" he said as he drank the poison.

The drug was quick. He placed his lips on Juliet's once more. "With this kiss, I die."

His body shook and then he died.

"Who's in here?" called Friar Lawrence as he entered the tomb.

He lifted his torch and saw Paris dead on the ground. Then he saw Romeo dead at the base of the stone where Juliet was lying.

"If only I had been here one hour earlier, then I could have saved them both," he mumbled[2].

Juliet groaned. "And now the lady awakes!"

Juliet rose up and saw Friar Lawrence. "Friar," she said. "Where is my husband?

Horses could be heard in the distance[3]. "I hear some noise," said Friar Lawrence. "Let's leave right away!"

1. **fall to one's knees** 跪下
2. **mumble** ['mʌmbəl] (v.) 喃喃自語
3. **in the distance** 在遠處

Short answer question.

What is the last thing Romeo does before he dies?

____

Ans: He kisses Juliet.

47

"Where is Romeo?" demanded[1] Juliet.

They could hear voices coming closer.

"I cannot stay!" whimpered[2] Friar Lawrence. "Romeo is dead on the ground. Paris is also dead. Now come on!"

"You may go," she said, kneeling to examine[3] Romeo.

"My lady, I have to go!"

"Then go," Juliet said, "but I cannot."

Friar Lawrence looked at Juliet and then ran out of the tomb.

"What's this?" thought Juliet. "A bottle in Romeo's hand? It's poison."

She looked at the bottle. "You drank it all and didn't leave any for me." She took the knife from Romeo's belt.

"I cannot live without Romeo," she said, and she stuck the knife into her heart.

1. **demand** [dɪˈmænd] (v.) 查問
2. **whimper** [ˈwɪmpər] (v.) 啜泣（抽噎）地說
3. **examine** [ɪgˈzæmɪn] (v.) 細查

She fell on top of Romeo just as the prince rushed in. Montague followed him in, and so did Capulet and his wife.

"The peace in my city has been broken." The prince looked at the two old men. "I'm sure that this is because of the hate you have between your two families."

Check Up

How does Juliet kill herself?

- [a] She jumps from the top of the tomb.
- [b] She drinks some of the poison from Romeo's bottle.
- [c] She uses Romeo's knife.

Ans: c

48

More torches were brought in.

"What happened here?" demanded the prince.

A captain entered and whispered into the prince's ear.

The prince nodded. "All right, then. Bring the suspicious[1] man in."

Two soldiers dragged[2] in Friar Lawrence and threw him on the ground.

Friar Lawrence pleaded[3], "I know I look guilty[4], but I didn't murder anyone."

"Then what happened here?" asked the prince.

Friar Lawrence told them everything. He told them how he had married Romeo and Juliet.

Everyone gasped.

"When old Capulet said he wanted her to marry Paris she came to me for help," said Friar Lawrence. "I gave her a drink to make her sleep. She would have killed herself there in my room if I hadn't."

1. **suspicious** [sə'spɪʃəs] (a.) 可疑的
2. **drag** [dræg] (v.) 拉；拖
3. **plead** [pli:d] (v.) 辯護
4. **guilty** ['gɪlti] (a.) 有罪的
5. **get *A* to** 說服A……

"Continue," said the prince.

"I tried to tell Romeo, but my letter arrived too late. When I came here to get Juliet, Romeo had already arrived. He didn't know that she was just sleeping, so he killed himself."

He looked at Paris' body. "I guess Paris died trying to stop Romeo from entering the tomb. I tried to get Juliet to[5] leave, but she wouldn't."

"Why didn't you stay with her?" asked Capulet.

"I was afraid. I'm a coward," he cried.

"Enough," the prince said. "It's true that you should have helped these young people. But it's not your fault[1]," said the prince.

He turned to Capulet and Montague. "See what has happened because of your ancient[2] grudge[3]. You've lost your only children."

Capulet looked up from the body of his daughter. He saw his old enemy kneeling across from him. "Brother Montague," he said, "please forgive me for all of this hatred[4]."

Montague leaned across the bodies of Romeo and Juliet and put his arms around Capulet. "I will make a pure gold statue[5] in honor of[6] your daughter."

"And I will put one of Romeo by her side."

Prince Escalus lifted the two old men to their feet. "Let's leave this place and talk somewhere else."

He led all the grieving[7] people out of the tomb. "There has never been a more tragic[8] story than this one of Romeo and Juliet," said the prince.

1. **fault** [fɔːlt] (n.) 過錯
2. **ancient** [ˈeɪnʃənt] (a.) 古代的；舊的
3. **grudge** [grʌdʒ] (n.) 怨恨
4. **hatred** [ˈheɪtrɪd] (n.) 憎恨
5. **statue** [ˈstætʃuː] (n.) 雕像
6. **in honor of** 紀念……
7. **grieving** [ˈɡriːvɪŋ] (a.) 悲傷的
8. **tragic** [ˈtrædʒɪk] (a.) 悲慘的；不幸的

Comprehension Quiz Chapters Five & Six

A Fill in the blanks with the given words.

disobey tomb potion hobbled numb

1. Tybalt's dead body was placed in the family __________.
2. Juliet drank a __________ made of flowers.
3. Juliet's body went __________ after drinking the potion.
4. Juliet wanted to __________ her father and not to marry Paris.
5. Capulet __________ around because he was so old.

B True or False.

T F 1. The monk gave Romeo a letter in Mantua.

T F 2. Romeo wanted to kill Paris because he loved Juliet.

T F 3. The prince thought Capulet and Montague was to blame for all the trouble.

T F 4. Friar Lawrence arrived too late to save Romeo.

T F 5. Capulet and Montague wouldn't apologize to each other.

C Choose the correct answer.

1. Why did Lady Capulet think Juliet was crying?
   (a) Because she had to marry Paris.
   (b) Because of Tybalt's death.
   (c) Because of that villain Romeo

2. Why did Friar Lawrence run away from the tomb?
   (a) He was trying to get help.
   (b) Juliet ordered him to leave.
   (c) He was afraid.

D Rearrange the sentences in chronological order.

1. Juliet asks Friar Lawrence for help.
2. Romeo visits Juliet's bedroom.
3. The nurse finds Juliet in a death-like sleep.
4. Juliet's parents order her to marry Paris.
5. Juliet feels betrayed by her nurse.

_____ ⇨ _____ ⇨ _____ ⇨ _____ ⇨ _____

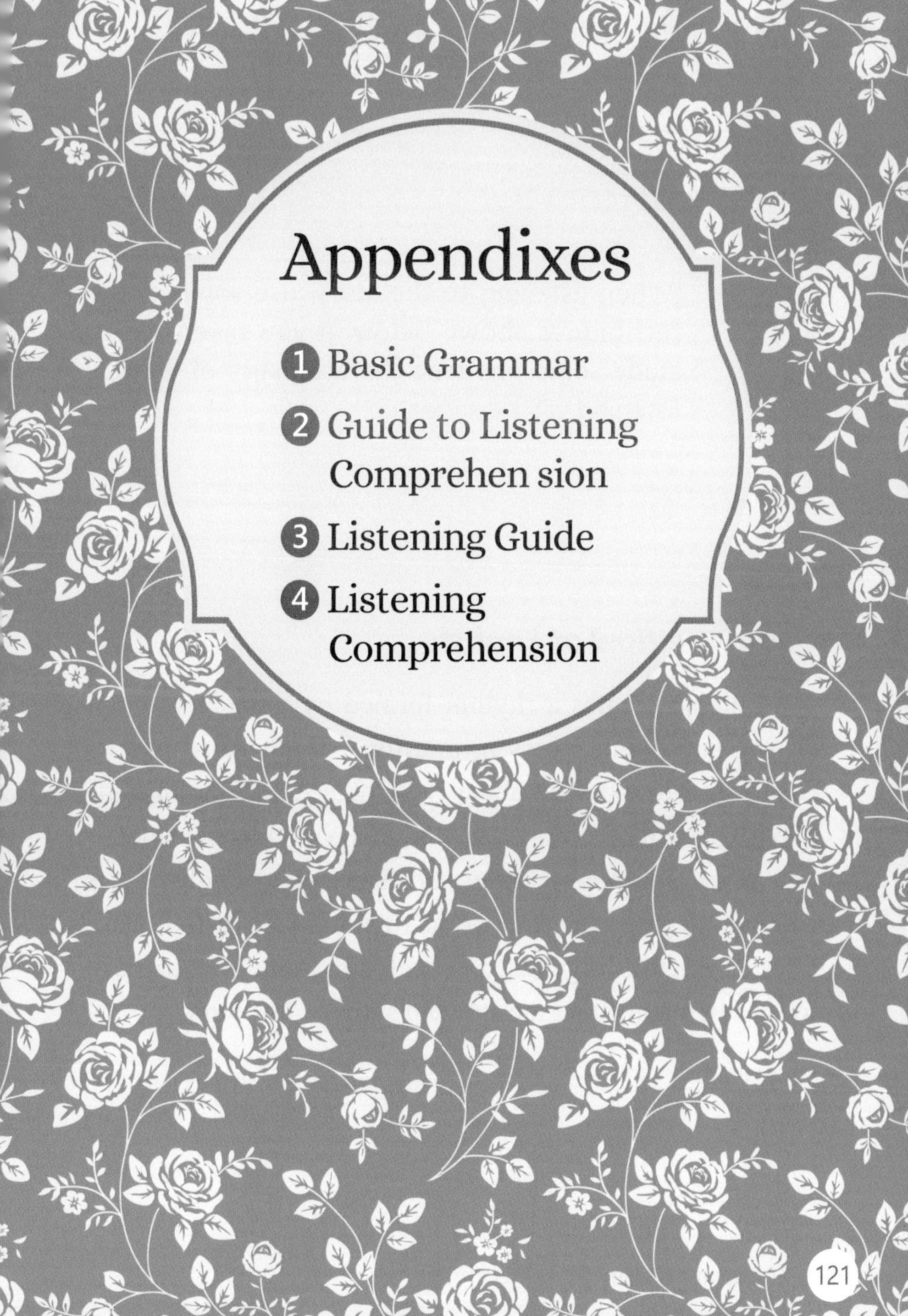

Appendixes

1. Basic Grammar
2. Guide to Listening Comprehen sion
3. Listening Guide
4. Listening Comprehension

Appendix 1

Guide to Listening Comprehension

When listening to the story, use some of the techniques shown below. If you take time to study some phonetic characteristics of English, listening will be easier.

Get in the flow of English.

English creates a rhythm formed by combinations of strong and weak stress intonations. Each word has its particular stress that combines with other words to form the overall pattern of stress or rhythm in a particular sentence.

When you are speaking and listening to English, it is essential to get in the flow of the rhythm of English. It takes a lot of practice to get used to such a rhythm. So, you need to start by identifying the stressed syllable in a word.

Listen for the strongly stressed words and phrases.

In English, key words and phrases that are essential to the meaning of a sentence are stressed louder. Therefore, pay attention to the words stressed with a higher pitch. When listening to an English recording for the first time, what matters most is to listen for a general understanding of what you hear. Do not try to hear every single word. Most of the unstressed words are articles or auxiliary verbs, which don't play an important role in the general context. At this level, you can ignore them.

Pay attention to liaisons.

In reading English, words are written with a space between them. There isn't such an obvious guide when it comes to listening to English. In oral English, there are many cases when the sounds of words are linked with adjacent words.

For instance, let's think about the phrase "**take off**," which can be used in "take off your clothes." "Take off your clothes" doesn't sound like [teɪk ɔːf] with each of the words completely and clearly separated from the others. Instead, it sounds as if almost all the words in context are slurred together, [ˋteɪkɔːf], for a more natural sound.

Shadow the voice of the native speaker.

Finally, you need to mimic the voice of the native speaker. Once you are sure you know how to pronounce all the words in a sentence, try to repeat them like an echo. Listen to the book again, but this time you should try a fun exercise while listening to the English.

This exercise is called "shadowing." The word "shadow" means a dark shade that is formed on a surface. When used as a verb, the word refers to the action of following someone or something like a shadow. In this exercise, pretend you are a parrot and try to shadow the voice of the native speaker.

Try to mimic the reader's voice by speaking at the same speed, with the same strong and weak stresses on words, and pausing or stopping at the same points.

Experts have already proven this technique to be effective. If you practice this shadowing exercise, your English speaking and listening skills will improve by leaps and bounds. While shadowing the native speaker, don't forget to pay attention to the meaning of each phrase and sentence.

Listen to what you want to shadow many times. Start out by just trying to shadow a few words or a sentence.

Mimic the CD out loud. You can shadow everything the speaker says as if you are singing a round, or you also can speak simultaneously with the recorded voice of the native speaker.

As you practice more, try to shadow more. For instance, shadow a whole sentence or paragraph instead of just a few words.

Listening Guide

Chapter One page 10–11 50

"I will not fight," said Sampson, "but nobody should insult me. If we see any Montagues, they (❶) ( ) be quiet."

"Or what?" asked Gregory.

"I'll kill them all."

"All?" Gregory (❷) ( ) and looked at his friend.

"Every one of them," said Sampson. "If they are Montagues, then I'll fight them if they say something to me."

They began to walk on toward the square.

"(❸) ( ) one of the Montagues' dogs barks at you?" Gregory asked jokingly.

"Then I'd fight with it."

"What about women?"

This time Sampson stopped, as if to (❹) ( ) the question. "It's all the same. If they are Montagues, they are my enemies. And they will know I'm angry."

"So you'd fight with the women?"

"I didn't say that," Sampson explained. "I said they'd know I'm angry. I'd fight with the men. After beating them, I would be (❺) ( ) the women."

以下為《羅密歐與茱麗葉》各章節的前半部。一開始若能聽清楚發音，之後就沒有聽力的負擔。先聽過摘錄的章節，之後再反覆聆聽括弧內單字的發音，並仔細閱讀各種發音的說明。以下都是以英語的典型發音為基礎，所做的簡易說明，即使這裡未提到的發音，也可以配合音檔反覆聆聽，如此一來聽力必能更上層樓。

❶ **had better:** had 發音為 [hæd]，因其字尾是有聲子音 [d]，而 better 的字首 b 是子音發音；為求講話發音的流暢，在口語連音中往往不發出 [d] 的音，而是做一個快速的頓音滑過去。

❷ **stopped walking:** 動詞 stop 的字尾是無聲子音 [p]，所以過去式字尾「-ed」，發音成 [t]，stopped 讀成 [stɑːpt]。但為求講話發音的流暢，在口語連音中往往不發 [t] 的音，而是做一個快速的頓音滑過去，唸成 [ˈstɑːpˈwɔːkɪŋ]。

❸ **what if:** what 的字尾為無聲子音 [t]，後面接 if 一起發音時，為了口語連音，[t] 通常省略不發音。所以，唸起來為 [wɑːɪf]。

❹ **think about:** about 發音為 [əˈbaʊt]，它的字首 a 發短母音，所以這兩個單字在口語連音時，讀成 [θɪŋkəˈbaʊt]。

❺ **kind to:** kind 的字尾是有聲子音 [d]，而其後面的 to 為子音發音，為求講話發音的流暢，在口語連音中往往不發出 [d] 的音，而是做一個快速的頓音滑過去。

"You mean you'd charm them? Once the Montague men were gone?"

"Yes, I guess so."

"But that's not really showing them that you're angry. Unless you think charming the women is the same as fighting the men."

"(❶) ( )" Sampson answered. "Either way, it's about showing the Montagues who's the boss. I'll beat the men with swords, the women with smiles and pretty words. It's all the same."

"I wish it were the same," said Gregory, seeing two servants from the Montague family (❷) from across the square. "Then you could (❸) ( ) and say kind things to these two and be satisfied."

Sampson watched the two men strut through the square. "I can think of nothing kind to say."

The two men began to walk toward Sampson and Gregory, looking at them with angry eyes. They were making nasty remarks among themselves about Sampson and Gregory.

Gregory gave an unnatural smile as the two passed by. Sampson did the same, but he (❹) ( ) hold in his hatred. (❺) ( ) ( ) the men passed, he stuck out his middle finger and went, "AARRRRRRR!"

❶ **Isn't it?**：這是一個疑問句，所以發音結束時語氣要上揚。也就是說，唸到 it 時，語調提高。

❷ **approaching**：approaching 音標 [ə'proʊtʃɪŋ]。字首 a 發短母音，所以重音在後。

❸ **just smile**：just 的 -t 為無聲子音，後面接著 smile 一起發音時，為了發口語連音，[t] 通常省略不發音；而 smile 的字首 s 也為無聲子音，兩個 s 只發一個 [s] 的音。所以，唸起來為 jusmile。

❹ **could not**：could 發音為 [kʊd]，因其字尾是有聲子音 [d]，而 could 後面的 not 為子音發音，為求講話發音的流暢，在口語連音中往往不發出 [d] 的音，而是做一個快速地頓音滑過去。

❺ **As soon as**：這個片語連音讀起來變成 [əz'suːnˌəz]。

Appendix 3

Listening Comprehension

52 **A** Listen to the CD. Write down the questions and fill in the blanks.

1. They were making __________ __________ among themselves.
2. Would you rather see me in hate? Montagues love to __________, __________, and __________.
3. Juliet is perfect, and it is __________ to love __________, right?
4. A marriage would __________ __________ between the __________ families.
5. Romeo's __________ and can never come back.

53 **B** Listen to the CD. Write down the sentences and names.

Juliet | Friar Lawrence | the prince | Romeo

1. ______________________________ (   )
2. ______________________________ (   )
3. ______________________________ (   )
4. ______________________________ (   )

C Listen to the CD. Write down the questions and choose the correct answer.

1 ______________________________?

(a) On the balcony.
(b) At the church.
(c) At the party.

2 ______________________________?

(a) On the balcony.
(b) At the church.
(c) At the party.

54

D Listen to the CD. Write down the sentences and circle either True or False.

T F 1 ______________________________

T F 2 ______________________________

T F 3 ______________________________

T F 4 ______________________________

T F 5 ______________________________

作者簡介 p. 2

威廉·莎士比亞（William Shakespeare, 1564–1616）出生於英國的中產家庭，是舉世聞名的劇作家。莎士比亞的童年因家境富裕而安逸舒適，然 13 歲時因家道中落而未能念大學。

18 歲時他與長他 8 歲的安·海瑟薇（Anne Hathaway）結婚，育有三子。據說莎士比亞約在 1590 年開始成為劇作家。一開始，他只練習寫作，摘取他人故事的想法。然而他勤奮努力並日漸出名，最終以演員與劇作家的身分獲得成功，並在 1594 年成為皇家官方劇團的成員之一，在此持續寫作直至終老。

他著有 37 個劇本，作品被廣泛分為四個時期：歷史劇時期、「歡樂」（joyous）喜劇時期、悲劇時期與悲劇浪漫喜劇時期。他著名的四大悲劇為《哈姆雷特》（*Hamlet*）、《奧賽羅》（*Othello*）、《李爾王》（*King Lear*）與《馬克白》（*Macbeth*），寫於悲劇時期。莎劇中的十四行詩使他享有詩人之首的頭銜，及有史以來最偉大劇作家的名聲。

1616 年 4 月 23 日，莎士比亞在 52 歲生日當天於出生地史特拉福（Stratford-Upon-Avon）去世，當地居民至今仍年年為其冥誕慶祝。

故事介紹

p. 3

《羅密歐與茱麗葉》

故事場景設定在義大利的美麗城市維洛納，當地蒙特鳩家族與卡布萊兩大家族結為多年世仇。

某天，蒙特鳩家族的獨子羅密歐，偷偷混入卡布萊家族舉辦的舞會。在那裡，他遇見卡布萊家族的女兒茱麗葉，兩人一見鍾情。雖然他們知道彼此的家庭互為敵人，但仍不禁愛上對方。相遇隔天，他們便在修道院悄悄地成婚了。

而同時，茱麗葉的表親提伯特因為羅密歐現身舞會而暴跳如雷，宣告欲與羅密歐決鬥。羅密歐從婚禮的旅途歸來，便和提伯特發生衝突。考量現已與提伯特結為親戚，羅密歐便拒絕與其搏鬥。然而，提伯特最終傷害了羅密歐的朋友莫枯修，悲憤之下，羅密歐也殺了提伯特。

《羅密歐與茱麗葉》是寫於 1590 年中的劇作，共 5 幕 24 場。戲中使人興嘆的瑰麗詩句與年輕愛侶受世仇所害的命運，一同讓《羅密歐與茱麗葉》成為莎士比亞的佳作之一，同時也是他其中一部最常被搬上舞台的劇作。

人物介紹

p. 8–9

Romeo 羅密歐

我為我所愛的女人而活，她就是茱麗葉。我身邊還有其他女人出現，但對她們的記憶都已經在我腦海中消失，她才是我唯一的真愛。雖然我是蒙特鳩家族的人，而茱麗葉是卡布萊家族的人，但是我們的愛可以戰勝世仇。在我人生中，愛是最重要的，甚至比我的生命更重要。

Juliet 茱麗葉

喔！羅密歐，你在哪裡？彷彿是命運讓我與我的真愛分隔兩地。父親卡布萊爵爺要我嫁給貴族巴利斯，但我做不到。當我第一眼見到羅密歐，我就知道他是我的真命天子。我愛羅密歐更勝於我自己的生命！

Friar Lawrence 勞倫斯神父

現在的孩子把愛情看得太重了。羅密歐與茱麗葉想要結婚？他們太年輕了！他們的父親彼此憎恨！但或許，只是或許，他們的婚姻可以結束這兩個家族之間的仇恨。

Juliet's Nurse 茱麗葉的奶媽

我照顧茱麗葉這麼多年了，她就像是我的女兒一樣。如果羅密歐的愛不是真心的，那我必須保護茱麗葉，她才不會因為羅密歐而受傷。但是如果他是真心的，那他對茱麗葉來說會是個好丈夫。他是我見過最帥的人了。

Benvolio 班福留

我最近有很多煩惱。在我的蒙特鳩家族與世仇卡布雷家族之間，戰爭似乎隨時都會爆發。我也擔心我的堂弟羅密歐。他正在戀愛，而這場戀愛讓他很傷心。我必須想辦法來幫助他找回快樂。

[第一章] 世仇

p. 10–11「我不會挑釁，」桑普森說：「但是也沒有人可以侮辱我。如果讓我見到任何蒙特鳩家族的人，他們最好安靜點。」

「不然呢？」格雷戈里問。

「我會把他們全都殺了。」

「全部？」格雷戈里停下來，看著他的朋友。

「一個都不留。」桑普森說：「如果蒙特鳩家族的人對我說三道四的，我就會和他們對幹。」

他們走向了廣場。

「如果蒙特鳩家族養的狗對著你吠呢？」格雷戈里開玩笑地問。

「那我會跟牠打一場。」

「那要是女人呢？」

這次換桑普森停下來了，他好像在思考這問題似的，「都一樣。如果他們是蒙特鳩家族，那他們就是我的敵人。他們會知道我是不好惹的。」

「所以你會和女人對戰？」

「我不是那個意思，」桑普森解釋說：「我是說他們會知道我是不好惹的。我會和男人對戰，打贏他們後，我就會善待女人的。」

「你是說蒙特鳩家族的男人都消失了，你就會讓女人神魂顛倒嗎？」

「對啊，可以這麼說啦。」

p. 12–13 「但那並不真的表示你不好惹，除非你覺得讓女人神魂顛倒，和跟男人對戰這兩件事是一樣的。」

「不是嗎？不管是哪種方式，都是在告訴蒙特鳩家族的人，誰才是老大。我會用劍來打敗男人，用微笑和甜言蜜語來征服女人。都是一樣的。」桑普森說。

「希望是一樣的。」格雷戈里說。看著蒙特鳩家的兩個僕人正穿過廣場走過來，他又說道:「那你可以對這兩人只是微笑、說些好話，然後就感到心滿意足。」

桑普森看著這兩人趾高氣揚地走過廣場，說道：「我想不到半句好話可說。」

這兩人正朝著桑普森和格雷戈里走過來，怒氣沖沖地看著他們。他們用齷齪下流的語氣，評論著桑普森和格雷戈里。

那兩人經過時，格雷戈里不自然地笑著。桑普森也是，但他掩飾不住自己心中的敵意。等兩人走掉，他舉起中指發出「啊！啊！」的聲音。

p. 14–15 這兩人停下來轉過身。「你對我們比中指嗎？」其中一人問。

桑普森對著格雷戈里小聲的說：「呃，如果我說『是』，那法律上站得住腳嗎？」

「站不住腳。」

「那就是沒有。」桑普森說。

「但是我看到你伸出你的手指。」一名叫亞伯拉罕的人說。

「而且我還聽到你發出聲音。」另一個叫包薩澤的人說。

桑普森無辜地說：「我伸出手指，然後發出聲音。那又怎樣？」

「這就是卡布萊家族的人，是吧？」另一個人說。「對著老實人做出粗魯的舉動，卻又膽小不敢承認。」

「就是卡布萊家的人。」亞伯拉罕也附和說：「膽小鬼，個個都是。」

「沒道理叫人膽小鬼。」格雷戈里說。

「我來告訴你誰是膽小鬼吧。」桑普森說道。他一手抓起他的匕首，卻不小心把格雷戈里推向亞伯拉罕。

「包薩澤，你看到沒？他攻擊我。」亞伯拉罕大叫。

情況再也沒法保持平和了。四人在街頭扭打成一團。群眾聚集在一旁，開始大聲鼓譟。

p. 16–17 老蒙特鳩的姪子班福留聽到了打鬥聲。他不是很喜歡他的家族與卡布萊家族間的恩怨。他知道所有的怨恨都會走向死亡，而死亡又會帶來更多怨恨。

但是他知道唯一可以停止這場打鬥的方法，就是跳進這群氣憤的人當中，將他們隔開。於是他抽出劍，向廣場打鬥的那四人跑去。

「住手！放下你們的武器！」班福留拉開這些人大叫著說。

一個高大的人走向前。他抽出劍，摸了摸刀尖。

這是提伯特，卡布萊的姪子，是個三十歲的傲慢者。他非常自負，但也是維洛納城裡頂尖的劍術高手。

班福留說：「提伯特，把你的劍放下。我正在努力維持大家和睦，幫幫忙吧！」

「和睦？你手上拿著劍，站在這裡講和睦？」提伯特帶著詭異的微笑說。

提伯特撲向班福留，班福留幾乎來不及防衛自己。

群眾又再度鼓譟。有些人叫出：「殺死蒙特鳩的人！」

也有些人喊著：「殺死卡布萊的人！」

還有更多人大喊著：「把他們全都殺死！」

p. 18–19「殺死卡布萊？」一個正走出附近教堂的老人喃喃自語。

那是卡布萊，他握住年輕妻子的手臂說：「把我的劍給我！」

「劍？」他的妻子斥責：「你需要一支枴杖，可不是一把劍。」

「我知道那是卡布萊家族的人。」另一個老人踩著蹣跚的步伐穿過廣場，那是蒙特鳩。「帶我過去。」他說。

「你要怎麼打？你連走路都有問題了。」蒙特鳩夫人說。

當幾匹馬走近時，眾人突然安靜了下來。那是維洛納城的親王埃斯卡勒斯和士兵往他們騎來。他把提伯特跟班福留圍住，看熱鬧的人急忙閃開。

「你們想造反啦！」親王怒吼道：「把你們的武器丟下！」

提伯特和班福留遵照親王之命丟下。

埃斯卡勒斯親王說：「現在，該負責的人在哪兒？我說的是那兩個老卡布萊和老蒙特鳩。」

他目光搜尋街上，看到兩個老人。「你，卡布萊，你，蒙特鳩，給我站到面前來！」

這兩個老人邁步向前。「你們是這個城的領導者，應該是人品很高潔的，然而你們非但沒有教導大家成為高尚之士，反而把他們捲入你們毫無意義的恩怨中。好，我已經忍耐很久了。」

他抽出劍，「你們要是再讓恩怨擾亂街頭的寧靜，那就得付出命來！明白了嗎？」

兩人都點了點頭。

p. 20–21 當蒙特鳩家的人回到城堡時，蒙特鳩夫人問班福留說：「我的羅密歐沒有加入這場打鬥中吧？」

「沒有。」班福留說。

「如果羅密歐沒有和你在一起，那他在哪裡？」

「夫人，我最後一次看到他，是在今天早上。他靠在花園牆上，看起來很哀傷。」

「喔！我可憐的羅密歐。」蒙特鳩夫人緊握著自己的手，「你知道為什麼嗎？」

「夫人，我不知道。我走向他，但他跑掉了。」

「我也曾經看到他傷心地待在花園裡，我問了他原因，但他什麼都沒說。」蒙特鳩夫人傷心地笑著。

正當他們抵達城堡時，有個年輕人走出玫瑰叢。

「夫人，是羅密歐。」班福留說。

「要我再問他嗎？」

「拜託你了。」蒙特鳩夫人說。她拍拍班福留的手腕，便和丈夫一起離開了。

「早安，我的堂弟。」班福留說。

「現在還是早上嗎？」羅密歐說著，扔了顆石頭到噴泉裡。

「現在才九點。」

「悲傷的時光總是過得特別慢。」羅密歐又丟了一顆石頭。「為什麼時間好像這麼漫長？」

「我無法讓時間變得短一點。」

「你說的是愛，」班福留快活地說：「我想你八成戀愛了！」

p. 22–23 羅密歐丟了更多的石頭到噴泉裡，說：「外面！」

班福留不確定羅密歐的意思，是叫他走嗎？「羅密歐，你在說什麼？」

「外面！」他又說了一次，「我不是在談戀愛，而是在愛情之外。我愛的人不愛我，所以我是在愛情之外。」

班福留輕聲地笑著，他以為自己聽到了笑話，但羅密歐卻無意開玩笑。

「不要笑我！」他瞪著班福留。

「沒，沒有，」班福留說：「只是……」

羅密歐舉起手說：「原諒我，我因為想太多，已經一天沒睡了。」

然後他注意到班福留臉上的血。「我甚至沒注意到你受傷了。」

班福留說：「沒事的，只是和卡布萊家打個小架罷了。」

「我該和你一起的，也許我幫不上忙，但卡布萊家的人可以刺死我，讓我脫離痛苦。」

「你不是認真的吧！」

羅密歐的眼神流露出他的認真。

「我討厭看到你這樣。」

「討厭？」羅密歐大叫，抓著班福留。「討厭看到我在戀愛？所以你討厭我！」

他搖了搖堂哥，「或是你更想看到我沉浸在仇恨中？是這樣嗎？蒙特鳩家的人喜愛仇恨、爭鬥和殺戮。但是無論我們喜歡恨或是愛都無所謂，這都是同樣的激情，都會置我們於死地。」

p. 24–25 班福留並不喜歡羅密歐這樣說話，畢竟，他剛剛才冒著生命危險阻止了一場爭鬥。但是他知道羅密歐是對的，家族間的問題就是因為過度激情所致，他也知道羅密歐擁有同樣的激情。他想要幫助這堂弟。

「你能告訴我你愛的人是誰嗎？」

「一個女人。」他喃喃的說。

班福留說：「是啊！誰呢？」

「羅瑟琳。」羅密歐說。

「羅瑟琳？」班福留的神情都亮了，「那有譜了，我知道她今晚會參加一場卡布萊家舉辦的舞會。」

「在卡布萊家？父親的仇人？我進不去卡布萊家，我一定會被做掉，雖然那可能也不會太慘。」

「兄弟啊！」班福留說：「我們的朋友莫枯修受邀出席舞會，我們可以和他一起進去。我們會戴上面具，不會有人認出我們的啦。」

羅密歐看起來開心了點。

「死期還沒到，對吧？」班福留很高興看到羅密歐可以開心點，「但是我警告你，到時候那裡會有很多漂亮的女生，你就會忘記羅瑟琳了。」

「喔！班福留，不會有人比她更漂亮了，我也不想要別人。」

「相信你所要的。」班福留說：「去準備參加舞會吧！」

p. 26–27 卡布萊喝了幾口冷水，靠在椅背上，「我很高興蒙特鳩的人得跟我遵守同樣的規定，不管是誰破壞了和平都會死。」他笑著說：「破壞和平！這可有趣了！」

「為什麼？」他的親戚巴利斯問著。

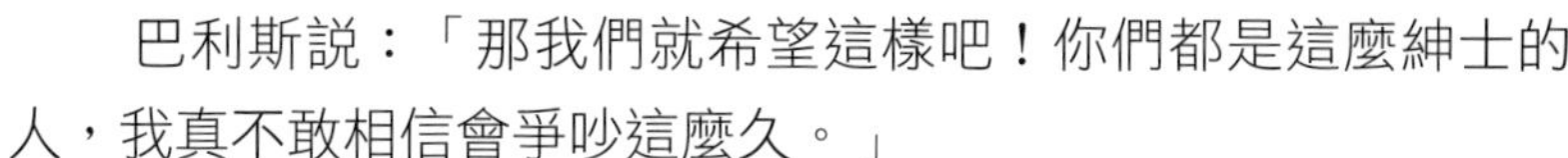

「因為我們兩個老到破壞不了和平了，像我們這樣的老人應該置身於爭鬥之外。」

「先生，您說得沒錯，但是家族的年輕人呢？他們生氣起來就沒長腦袋了。」

卡布萊說：「是啊！年輕人隨心不帶腦的想事情，但是他們會聽從長輩的話。」

巴利斯說：「那我們就希望這樣吧！你們都是這麼紳士的人，我真不敢相信會爭吵這麼久。」

「說實話，我自己甚至都忘了是怎麼開始的。」卡布萊又笑了。

巴利斯也笑了起來，但是他想換個話題，「你考慮過我請求的事了嗎？」

「你的請求？我都快忘了。」卡布萊說。

p. 28–29 「你反對這場聯姻嗎？」巴利斯問。

「不是。」卡布萊說：「雖然我也不是真的贊成。你是個優秀的年輕人，只是茱麗葉還這麼年輕，再給她兩年的時間吧！」

「許多比她年輕的女孩都已經當媽媽了。」巴利斯小心地提出異議。

「那是因為她們太早結婚了！」卡布萊高分貝地打斷。

但他知道巴利斯是對的。他結婚時太太也正好是茱麗葉的年紀，只是卡布萊還沒準備好要看著唯一的女兒出嫁，但是又找不到她不該出嫁的理由，畢竟她不可能永遠當他的小女孩。

巴利斯說：「我讓你煩心了吧，您是她父親，知道什麼才是對她最好的。」

「等一下。」卡布萊說。

巴利斯停住腳。

「我會同意這門婚事，但是最後的決定權在茱麗葉手上。」卡布萊說：「今晚來參加舞會，如果她願意嫁給你，那你就會得到我的祝福。」

「謝謝，我會的！」巴利斯大聲說著走出房間。

卡布萊獨自看著窗外，他想像著茱麗葉墜入愛河，就一如他以前一樣，然後便去休息了。

p. 34–35 維洛納城的街道

在《羅密歐與茱麗葉》中，莎士比亞將十四世紀的維洛納城，描繪成一個人們會為家族世仇在街頭械鬥的城市。而這實則為真，幾世紀來維洛納城一直陷入政治的紛擾不安，它在 1158 年陷入內戰，許多貴族效忠於天主教教宗，但也有不少貴族效忠於神聖羅馬帝國皇帝腓特烈一世。

雖在莎士比亞戲劇中從未言明蒙特鳩和卡布萊兩大家族的「世仇」究竟為何，但恩怨或可追溯到羅密歐與茱麗葉年代的兩百多年前。這些恩恩怨怨不只涉及了家族領導人，還包括兒女、堂兄弟姐妹，甚至僕人。

事實上，到今日維洛納城的許多貴族仍彼此仇恨。觀光客到維洛納城可發現上百棟老房子，都有厚重的圍牆和門禁森嚴的大門，這些房子從提伯特和莫枯修持械在街上晃的時代，就遺留下來了。

若以為羅密歐和茱麗葉的悲劇愛情，能終結這些世代恩怨，那就太過於不切實際了。雖然故事的時空有其歷史背景，但這篇故事單純只是虛構出來的。

[第二章] 一見鍾情

p. 32–33 「奶媽！」卡布萊夫人叫著。

「夫人，我來了。」奶媽喊著跑下樓梯。

「我女兒在哪兒？」卡布萊夫人質問道。

「我的小瓢蟲，妳在哪啊？茱麗葉！」奶媽朝著樓上大聲喊著。

茱麗葉現身樓梯上方，又長又黑的頭髮看起來好美。

卡布萊夫人說：「現在妳已經大到可以嫁人了，所以告訴我，茱麗葉，妳想要怎麼樣的婚禮？」

茱麗葉覺得這問題很棘手。她並不想讓母親失望，所以小心翼翼地回答：「結婚是我的夢想，」她委婉地說：「但現在談結婚還太早。」

卡布萊夫人知道這個問題不好處理，索性便直話直說：「我簡單地說，英勇的巴利斯想娶你。妳覺得如何，茱麗葉？」她接著說：「他今天晚上會出席舞會，好好觀察他一下再回答吧。」

「我會的。」茱麗葉答道。

卡布萊夫人看不出來茱麗葉是否開心，也不知道她到底會不會愛上巴利斯。

p. 34–35 「快點快點！」莫枯修對著羅密歐和班福留大叫：「我們快要遲到了。」

「我猜戀愛中的男人有丘比特的翅膀，應該可以飛起來吧。」莫枯修笑道。

「你錯了，莫枯修。」羅密歐說：「愛情是沈重的，所以愛人的腳步是緩慢的。」

「這是說你今晚沒辦法跳舞嗎？」莫枯修問，「如果我戀愛了我一定會跳舞的。」

「好了，我們沒時間聊，我們已經遲到了。我確定我們趕不上晚餐了，要是再不快一點連舞會也趕不上了。」班福留說。

羅密歐說：「遲到不會怎樣，怕的是，今晚會是場災難。」

「好吧！我們最好快一點。」莫枯修說：「我可不想讓戀愛中的男人倖免於難！」

他們匆匆走過街頭，來到大門口。在門另一頭偌大的大廳裡傳來音樂聲與笑聲。

「戴上面具吧！」莫枯修說：「否則門房不會放蒙特鳩家的人進去的。」

三個人戴著面具進入舞會。莫枯修和班福留跳起舞了，羅密歐在擁擠的人群中穿梭，希望見到心愛的羅瑟琳。

p. 36–37 然而羅密歐看到了另一個人。她猶如一幅畫，輕盈地移動著，彷如飄在空中。她真是太美了，美得像天使。

「她的美讓天上星星都閃亮了。」羅密歐喃喃自語。

他恍惚地走著。以前我真的愛過嗎？他問他自己。

「不！」他大聲回答：「不，今晚前我從未真正見過美女。」

他掀起面具，希望女孩看到他的臉。她看到了。

「怎麼了？」茱麗葉停下舞步，巴利斯問。

「沒事，有東西跑進眼睛裡了。」她說。

他們繼續跳舞，但是茱麗葉忍不住直瞧著剛見到的男孩。

他表哥也是。「我認得那張臉。」提伯特想。他不太記得在哪裡見過他，但覺得他貌似不錯的紳士。

他不停盯著那人看，慢慢記起在哪看過他了。就在廣場！提伯特發怒了。

「拿我的劍來！」提伯特對僕人咆哮。

僕人照辦。

「是蒙特鳩家的人！」提伯特生氣地說：「他戴著面具來我們的舞會，好來嘲笑我們！」

p. 38–39 「發生了什麼事？」卡布萊走過來問提伯特。

提伯特指著羅密歐說：「叔叔，他是蒙特鳩家的人。」

卡布萊看了一眼說：「是年輕的羅密歐。」

「羅密歐！」提伯特大叫。

「冷靜點，姪子，不要理他。」卡布萊說：「他現在看起來很規矩。耐心點，別管他。」

「來不及了。」提伯特說。

卡布萊不喜歡提伯特那麼魯莽，他想跟他講道理。

卡布萊說：「我看這樣就好，照我的意思吧，開心點，舞會上沒有不開心的人的。」

「舞會要是有敵人，人就不開心了。我受不了他出現這裡。」

「你要忍住！」卡布萊斥責說。

提伯特轉過身背對叔叔。

「你怎麼可以轉身背對著我？」卡布萊抓住提伯特，搖了搖他大叫說。

「這裡由我作主，我說，別管他了。」

「討厭！」提伯特嘀咕。

「是很討厭沒錯，不過你也太幼稚了。」卡布萊說。

「幼稚？我都已經三十歲了。」提伯特說。

「如果你給我的客人惹出麻煩來，還能說你是個男人嗎？」

他們嚷得很大聲，樂師停止了演奏，賓客也停下舞步。

p. 40–41 這時，巴利斯對茱麗葉說：「失禮了。如果我即將成為妳的丈夫，妳家族發生的事就會影響到我。我最好去瞧瞧發生了什麼事。」

「當然。」茱麗葉說。不過她根本沒聽清楚他說什麼。反正，他要走也是好。

卡布萊察覺到他們嚷得太大聲了。

「沒事，沒事。請繼續跳舞，好好玩！」他宣告。他捏了捏提伯特的臉頰，叫他去跳舞。

提伯特假裝沒事。他向叔叔鞠了個躬，就悻悻然走開。

在舞池上，茱麗葉聽到有聲音在她耳邊低語。

他說：「開始跳舞了。跟我來。」

「去哪？」她轉身看見羅密歐。即使被面具遮住，他仍然是她見過最帥的男子。

她跟著他來到一個隱密的角落。羅密歐拿下面具，握起茱麗葉的手。

「妳的手好輕柔，」他說：「妳好像天使，我真想溫柔地親吻妳。」

茱麗葉感覺血液直衝腦門，但她保持冷靜地說：「天使有翅膀，而且通常都會飛走。」她的手指輕扣羅密歐手指，然後緊緊地握住。

羅密歐顫抖著。茱麗葉的碰觸讓他感覺很奇妙。他更想要親吻她了，但是他還沒有得到茱麗葉的允許。

p. 42–43 「天使沒有雙唇嗎？」他撫摸著茱麗葉的手說道。

「有。」她回答。她知道羅密歐想親吻她，而她也想，但是她不想那麼隨便。茱麗葉知道年輕淑女要求陌生人親吻，一點也不恰當。但是他的撫摸是如此溫柔、堅定、溫暖，讓她幾乎可想像他的親吻是什麼感覺。

她要怎麼做才能讓他親吻她？羅密歐正在等她的回應。茱麗葉將眼神移開，害怕羅密歐會看穿她的心。

「我猜，妳的唇並不渴望一個吻。」他說著放開她的手。

但茱麗葉不想放開，她將羅密歐的手移到她的心房上。

羅密歐感覺到茱麗葉的心劇烈地乒砰跳。她看起來如此動人，他感覺如果他們的雙唇碰觸一起，他可能會融化。羅密歐不敢相信自己接下來所做出的事。

他吻了她。

「小姐！」奶媽大聲喊著，朝他們方向前來：「小姐，您的父親和巴利斯正在找您。」

茱麗葉跨出離開的步伐，但眼神仍停留在羅密歐身上。

羅密歐戴上面具。「她父親是誰？」

p. 44–45 奶媽認出了羅密歐，她回答：「那是茱麗葉，父親是這城堡主人。」

「她是卡布萊家的人？」羅密歐說。

「而你是…」

「單身貴族！」班福留打斷他們的談話，小聲說：「快，他們發現我們了，趁我們還沒鬧出事情前趕快離開。」

「我已經惹上麻煩了。」羅密歐說。

「那……那位紳士是誰？」茱麗葉問。

「他是我見過最帥的人。」奶媽回答。

「他結婚了嗎？」茱麗葉說。

「還沒，不過也可能結了。」

茱麗葉瞪著奶媽：「這是什麼意思？」

「他叫做羅密歐．蒙特鳩，是世仇的獨生子。」

「當然，他一定是蒙特鳩家族的人。」茱麗葉說。

她沒有解釋，只是深深地思念著羅密歐。她知道，就在剛剛，她的整個世界都改變了。她已經無法活在以前那個沒有羅密歐的世界裡。

羅密歐是宿敵的這事讓她更加激情。這時她知道有件事是很明白的，那就是——非改變不可的是他們的世界，而非他們的愛情。

茱麗葉說：「這麼說，我唯一的愛，來自於那唯一的世仇。」

「你說什麼？愛？」奶媽小聲的說：「我的寶貝墜入愛河了嗎？」

「茱麗葉！」遠處傳來一個聲音。那是巴利斯，還是父親的聲音，茱麗葉都無所謂了。

「告訴他們，我已經睡了。」

[第三章] 秘密婚禮

p. 48–49 羅密歐有些奇怪的想法，他沒辦法回家。他一定要再見到茱麗葉，但他又不能去她家，也沒其他地方可去。

夜裡，他又走回他父親敵人的家。他爬過花園圍牆，蹲在樹叢靜待著。

在上面點著蠟燭的房間裡，有個女子的身影。

「窗戶裡的人是誰？」羅密歐輕聲地說。

門慢慢地推開，茱麗葉站到陽台上。

「是我的天使！」羅密歐倒抽一口氣說：「喔，是我的愛！喔！但願她知道我有多麼愛她。」

茱麗葉將蠟燭放在陽台上。她凝視著黑夜，嘴唇喃喃地動著。

「她說話了。」羅密歐輕聲地說。

她說：「啊，是我！」

「喔！再說一次，我的天使！」羅密歐輕柔地說。

他可以看到她的氣息。他想要跑向她，爬上陽台，抱住她。但他擔心，她一旦知道他的名字就會討厭起他。

p. 50–51 茱麗葉又說話了：「喔！羅密歐，羅密歐，你在哪裡？我親愛的羅密歐，忘記你蒙特鳩的身分吧。要不，只要你說你愛我，我就不再是卡布萊家的人。」

羅密歐往後倒了下來。他死了嗎？這是天堂嗎？他站起來看了看，茱麗葉仍在那裡。

「我的敵人不過就是你的名字。」茱麗葉說：「但蒙特鳩算什麼？不過是個名字罷了。玫瑰花就算改名，聞起來依舊香甜。羅密歐，忘記你的名吧！你只屬於我。」

羅密歐再也忍不住。

「我只屬於妳！」他向前喊著說：「做我的愛人吧！那我便不再是羅密歐。」

「誰在那裡？」茱麗葉往後退，說道。

「我不知該如何告訴妳我的身分。」羅密歐說：「我討厭我的名，因那是妳仇家之名。」

「我沒聽清楚你說的話，但我認得這聲音。你是羅密歐，蒙特鳩家的人。你是怎麼進來的？」她問著：「怎麼可能？這牆很高，很難爬。如果被人發現你在這裡，你會有危險的。」

「為了愛，我跳過了牆。為了愛，人可不顧一切。」

愛！羅密歐說出了這個字。她盼他再說一次，但心又害怕。

「我怕你會被發現。」

「讓他們發現我吧！我寧可死在這裡，」羅密歐說：「也不願沒了妳的愛而悲慘地活著。」

她閉上眼睛，想像著他：「你愛我嗎？」她輕輕地問。

「我對妳的愛，言語無法形容！」羅密歐回答。

p. 52–53 「小姐！」房裡傳來一個聲音。是奶媽的聲音。

茱麗葉張大眼睛：「有聲音，快走，親愛的！」

羅密歐踮著腳走開，但茱麗葉並不希望他走:「不，別走！」

茱麗葉將身體伸出陽台外：「我該怎麼做才能讓你快樂？」

「妳可以把妳的心交給我，我也會給妳我的心。」

「早在你開口前我就把我的心交給你了。」茱麗葉微笑著，說道:「我對你的愛無限，深如大海，愛得越多，擁有的更多。」

「小姐！」奶媽大聲喊著。

「等一下！」茱麗葉喊道。

她對著羅密歐說：「若你的愛為真，想和我結婚，那就請明白告訴我。」

「我是真的想要和妳結婚。」羅密歐說。

「什麼時候？」

「明天，我會親自來。」羅密歐大膽地承諾。

「不，這太危險了。我會派奶媽去。你何時可備好？」茱麗葉說。

「明……明天九點。」

「感覺像要等二十年那般久，但我會忍耐，現在快走吧！」她說。

羅密歐離開了。

她送給羅密歐一個飛吻：「晚安，晚安。分離，是甜蜜的哀傷，然我明日即可見你了。」

他幾乎感覺到她的吻輕撫著自己的唇。

「在見到你前我都不會睡。」他說，然後消失在黑夜裡。

p. 54–55 勞倫斯神父正在花園裡工作。「啊！」他聞了聞鮮花的氣味，心想「土地是如此的美好，孕育了新生的花朵樹木。」

他從口袋裡拿出一把剪刀修剪花朵，哼著歌，一邊工作。

「早安，神父。」一個焦急的聲音傳來。

勞倫斯神父轉身看見羅密歐，說：「孩子，你怎麼起這麼早？我沒見過年輕人這麼早起的。」他親切地笑著：「還是你昨晚根本沒睡？」

「我是沒睡，但我有了最香甜的休息。」

「你是和羅瑟琳在一起，所以都沒睡？」羅倫斯神父問。

「羅瑟琳？我都忘了她了。」

「那很好，孩子。那你去哪了？」

「和我的敵人一起共舞！」羅密歐興奮地吶喊著。

「在那地方，我遺忘了羅瑟琳，領悟到什麼是真愛。」

勞倫斯神父揉了揉眼睛。

「你把我給搞糊塗，羅密歐，講明白點。」他說：

「我愛上了卡布萊家的女兒，」羅密歐說:「而且她也愛我。我們才剛認識，但我倆的愛至死不渝，我們已經互訂終生了。您今天一定要幫我們證婚。」

「幫你們證婚？」勞倫斯神父搖搖頭說：「只在昨日你還為羅瑟琳哭泣，今日卻要與他人另結婚約？」

p. 56–57 「您不是罵我不該愛羅瑟琳的嗎？」

「我罵你是因為你太迷她了。」

「你不是要我不要愛上她嗎？」

「是啊，但你也不該這麼快就愛上別人。你被感情沖昏頭了。」

「人不是有激情才活著嗎？」

「我們靠理性而活。」勞倫斯神父堅持，「因激情而死。」

「那麼讚美我的理性吧！我現在知道羅瑟琳這事您是對的，我並沒有愛上她。茱麗葉才是完美的，愛上完美之人是明智的吧？您一定要為我們證婚。」

勞倫斯神父望著日出，不敢相信自己所聽。他怎麼可以替如此年輕天真之人證婚？何況未經父母同意。

「神父？」羅密歐不耐地問著。

神父沒有回應，他繼續思索著。或許，一段婚姻可以促成兩個世仇家族和平。

「你還沒有說服我，羅密歐。」勞倫斯神父最後說：「但是我會為你們證婚，希望這段婚姻會為你們兩家帶來愛，而不是仇恨。」

勞倫斯神父將剪刀收回口袋，領著羅密歐走進教堂。

p. 58–59 「羅密歐到哪去了？」莫枯修靠在教堂階梯上：「你說你回到家時他不在家。」

「他不在，」班福留說，「不過提伯特派人送信給他。」。

「他在下戰帖嗎？」莫枯修問。

班福留踢了踢石頭：「我猜羅密歐一定會接下戰帖的。」

「那羅密歐小命不保了，提伯特是個很厲害的高手。」莫枯修說。

班福留知道莫枯修所言極是，但羅密歐可也不是懦夫。

若提伯特下了戰帖，羅密歐會接受，而且會死在提伯特劍下。班福留不想再想下去了。

「若知道羅密歐在哪兒，我會好過些。」班福留說。

「我們可憐的情聖來了。」莫枯修指著羅密歐說。

「羅密歐！」班福留喊。

「你昨晚怎麼和我們走散了？」莫枯修問。

「對不起，我有很重要的事要辦。」羅密歐說：「你們在擔心什麼？」

「擔心我們的朋友啊！」莫枯修說，「他最近為愛所苦，我們猜他可能做了什麼傻事了。」

「羅密歐，你看到信了嗎？」班福留問。

「什麼信？」

「從你的敵人卡布萊家送來的信。」班福留說。

羅密歐眼睛都亮了：「卡布萊家的信！信上寫了什麼？」

p. 60–61 「你在興奮什麼？」班福留問。

「這能算是新聞嗎？我戀愛了！」羅密歐問：「自從我上次聽到她的聲音好像有千年之久了。信在哪裡？」

「『她的聲音』是什麼意思？」班福留困惑地問。

「他瘋了，我也瘋了吧。」莫枯修揉揉眼睛，說：「有大象跑過來嗎？」

他們抬頭看見茱麗葉的奶媽正朝著他們走來。

「喔，我知道了，」莫枯修說，大聲到連奶媽都聽到了：「是個胖女人。」

「胖女人！」奶媽氣得漲紅臉向莫枯修跑去：「你很沒禮貌！」

「停！你們倆都冷靜點。」班福留大叫。

「我是來找年輕人羅密歐的，但看到他竟跟這般無禮之徒為伍，真是令人難過。」奶媽說。

「那妳把他帶走吧，」莫枯修說：「戀愛中的人不該和我們這種粗魯之士混在一起的。」

「找我什麼事，奶媽？」羅密歐問。

「我可以私下跟您談一談嗎？」奶媽問。

他們站到一旁去。

奶媽打量了羅密歐：「我家小姐把事情全告訴我了。她差我送口信來給您。但是首先，她還這麼年輕，您是假意愛她的吧？」

「假意？」羅密歐抗議：「我怎能假裝，因為茱麗葉，我找到我自己。我的感情、我的理性、我的靈魂，全都屬於她。」

奶媽不再懷疑羅密歐。她望著羅密歐深邃的眼睛，他是那麼地俊俏。

p. 62–63 羅密歐打斷了奶媽的凝視，說：「妳滿意我的回答嗎？」

奶媽滿臉泛紅。「我家小姐愛您，她是我的心肝寶貝，她的事就是我的事。喔！羅密歐，」她說，「您一定要讓茱麗葉很幸福。」

羅密歐微笑。「這正是我意。我和勞倫斯神父談過了，他同意為我們證婚。請安排一下，把茱麗葉帶來教堂讓我們完婚。」

「結婚？」奶媽說：「多美好啊！」

「儘快帶她來吧。」

茱麗葉在房裡來回踱步著，焦急不已。

「我派她去了這麼久，怎麼這麼慢啊？」她想。

她坐下，又站起。奶媽已去了三個多小時了。走到廣場要多久啊？

門被風吹開，茱麗葉聽到樓梯傳來腳步聲。

「喔，她回來了！」茱麗葉叫著。

她打開房門：「喔，怎麼樣？」她乞求著：「妳見到他了嗎？為何妳看來如此難過？」

p. 64–65 「等一下，」奶媽爬上樓梯時說：「我快要喘不過氣了。」

茱麗葉搖晃著奶媽：「告訴我！是好消息，還是壞消息？」

奶媽捏了捏她的臉頰：「您說他的臉俊美無比，但他的手、他的腳、他整個人更是完美無暇。」

奶媽倒在床上。

茱麗葉跳到她身上：「我知道，我知道！」她大叫著：「他有提到結婚的事嗎？」

「他是說了一點。」

「喔，妳在鬧我！」茱麗葉喊著：「我今天到底有沒有要結婚？」

奶媽露齒而笑。

「您不急著嫁給巴利斯，那為何您那麼急切想嫁給羅密歐？」

茱麗葉站起來挺直身，「我不是急。」，她說：「羅密歐到底怎麼說？」

「妳今天去告解了嗎？」

「別再戲弄我了！告訴我羅密歐到底說了什麼！」

茱麗葉很洩氣，倒向床上。

奶媽看她很可憐，「好吧，好吧，我只是捉弄一下。即將結婚的女子可以原諒我了。」她笑著說。

「結婚？」這字眼在茱麗葉腦中迴盪著。

「若您要告解的話，就得現在去教堂才行。到那裡，妳會找到一個急著跟您結婚的人。」她又笑了。

茱麗葉倒抽一口氣，抱著奶媽：「謝謝，謝謝妳！」她大叫：「現在就走吧！」

p. 66–67 勞倫斯神父正在幫羅密歐準備婚禮。他不確定這場婚禮是否得宜。未經得父母授意為兩個年輕人證婚，是為不妥；但他又盼望這場婚姻可拉近兩家的距離，只是不知是否能如願。

「他們會生氣嗎？會把氣出在我身上嗎？」他想著。

「我準備好了。」羅密歐說。他沒耐心再等候勞倫斯神父。

「冷靜點，羅密歐。」勞倫斯神父責備。

「生活和愛都要懂得節制，否則愛情或生命都不會長久。」

但他知道羅密歐冷靜不下來，茱麗葉也是。這時，茱麗葉朝著教堂跑來。

「我該把他們兩人都送回家。」勞倫斯神父想，但他明白自己不能這麼做。

「午安，神父。」茱麗葉唱道，跳進羅密歐懷裡。

「茱麗葉！」羅密歐抱著她：「請告訴我，妳愛我就如我愛妳一樣深！還有在我們婚後，妳會有多幸福。」

「我對你的愛，筆墨無法形容！」她親吻著他說。

「好，夠了。」勞倫斯神父將兩人分開，說：「趕快進行婚禮吧！」

p. 68–69 勞倫斯神父將他們帶到聖壇前，迅速進行結婚儀式。完畢，他讓兩人留下禱告，自己到花園去沈思。

奶媽在那裡找到了神父，說：「茱麗葉的家庭並不歡迎羅密歐，羅密歐的家庭也是。他們該怎麼辦？」

「我沒想到這點，或許他們可儘快讓父母知道。」勞倫斯神父答。

「神父，他們是新婚夫妻，想要待在一起。」奶媽笑道。

「妳就像茱麗葉的媽媽一樣，妳該在婚禮前就想到這問題的。」勞倫斯神父厲聲責怪。

「是您為他們證婚的，您也該想到這問題才對。」她說。

「他們需要我們的幫忙，我們該如何解決這問題？」神父問。

「他們的家長要是知道了這事，會把我們兩個給殺了。我們要先保密一陣子，先給這兩人有時間享受新婚生活。我想，過一陣子就會沒事的。」

「好吧，先帶茱麗葉回家。」勞倫斯神父同意。「今晚我會想法子讓羅密歐進去茱麗葉房間，這樣應可以先解決一陣子，之後我們再來擔心他們父母的事。」

p. 74–75 《羅密歐與茱麗葉》中的愛情、仇恨和命運

在《羅密歐與茱麗葉》中，莎士比亞探討了許多主題，其中最重要的就是愛情、仇恨和命運。

莎士比亞向讀者展示了多種不同類型的愛情，其中在此劇中提到的是「迷戀」，有時這愛情也稱「純純的愛」。

許多青少年會墜入此種愛情中，卻未曾發現它其實只是一種迷戀，並非真愛。羅密歐對於羅塞琳的愛便是一例。最重要的是，在此劇中可看到真愛，這種愛如此強烈到羅密歐與茱麗葉甚至可為愛犧牲生命。

莎士比亞也告訴讀者「仇恨」的重要課題。仇恨總會導致悲劇發生，就如《羅密歐與茱麗葉》中不必要的傷亡。當卡布萊與蒙特鳩家族從孩子死亡學到教訓時，已然太遲。

最後，莎士比亞強調了命運的概念。在劇初，作者提到羅密歐與茱麗葉是「命運乖舛」的戀人，表示兩人怎麼做都逃脫不了命運，註定無法幸福相守。羅密歐和茱麗葉起而對抗命運，為了要相守一起做了大膽之事。只是，結局卻仍擺脫不了已註定好的命運。

[第四章] 廣場之戰

p. 72–73 信差帶口信給班福留，是卡布萊家送來的。他們在找羅密歐。

「提伯特真的很生氣。」班福留告訴莫枯修說。

「我覺得我們應該離開這裡。」

「我不走。」莫枯修說。

「等他們來我不想在這裡。」班福留堅持：「我不想惹禍上身。」

這時，班福留看到提伯特和朋友正走過街道。

「喔，不！卡布萊家的人來了，快走！」班福留說。

「我才不怕他們。」莫枯修說。

太慢了，已經走不了了。

「午安！我可以和你們哪個聊聊嗎？」提伯特說。

「和我們聊聊？」莫枯修說：「這種找人打架的方式實在太怪了。」

「給我個理由，我就和你打。」提伯特手放劍上，說：「莫枯修，羅密歐昨晚和你在一起吧？他現在人呢？」

「我看起來像奴才嗎？」莫枯修說：「我該回答你每個問題嗎？就算我知道羅密歐在哪裡，我也不會告訴你的。」

提伯特抽出劍。

「紳士們，」班福留打斷他們：「停止打鬥，否則就到別處去打，大家都在看我們了。」

p. 78–79 「不需要。」提伯特說。他看到羅密歐正朝著他們走來。「我的人來了。」

「你的人？」莫枯修嘲諷著提伯特說：「他是你的僕人嗎？」

「講錯了，」羅密歐走近時，提伯特說。

「我該叫他壞蛋才對！」他看著羅密歐。

羅密歐只笑了笑，說：「提伯特，我愛你，所以我原諒你的憤怒。你很快就會明白我不是壞蛋。那現在就先再見了。」

提伯特認為羅蜜歐只是在嘲弄他。「你的出現毀了昨晚的舞會。現在轉身，抽出你的劍！」提伯特大叫說。

「我永遠都不會傷害你的，提伯特，而現在也不會，我愛你如同兄弟，比你所知更像兄弟。」他彎腰鞠躬：「開心點。」

莫枯修看著羅密歐，說：「他真無恥，他在演哪齣戲啊？」

「他有他的道理吧，靜靜離開這裡，開心點。」班福留說。

「要是提伯特死了我就會開心點。」莫枯修說。

提伯特舉起劍：「我已經準備好了等你來！」

「提伯特！莫枯修！」羅密歐說：「放下你們的劍！」

莫枯修把羅密歐推一旁，朝提伯特刺過去。提伯特腳步跨開，對莫枯修揮劍。

「提伯特！莫枯修！親王已下令禁止打鬥了！停下來！」羅密歐大叫：「班福留，幫我一起阻止打鬥。」

羅密歐站兩人中間，抓著莫枯修，但提伯特持續逼近。莫枯修想要防衛，羅密歐緊緊抓住他。這時，提伯特的劍刺入莫枯修胸口。

p. 76–77 「啊！」莫枯修哀叫著倒在地上。

提伯特抽出劍，擦掉上面的血。

班福留跑向莫枯修：「還好嗎？」

「很糟。」莫枯修咳了咳，手放胸前，血從指縫間噴出來。

「撐著點，你不會有事的。」羅密歐說。

「不，」莫枯修說著，逐漸失去知覺：「我快死了。」

血開始從他的口中冒出：「羅密歐，你為什麼要站在我們中間？害我防衛不了。」

羅密歐看著他的眼睛：「我是要阻止你們。」

「好，你阻止了我，」莫枯修喘著氣說：「讓他殺了我。」

「我要帶他去看醫生。」班福留說。他準備抬起莫枯修，但發現他已沒有了脈搏。

「他死了。」他說。

羅密歐瞪著莫枯修：「朋友因我而死。」他想，「提伯特嘲笑我們。喔！茱麗葉，願我們晚一天結婚，提伯特就不會成為我的兄弟，我就能為莫枯修報仇了。」

羅密歐極度憤怒，先前感受的愛與溫柔開始消失。瞬間，他忘了茱麗葉，忘了他的婚姻和未來。他想要正義，想要報仇。

他拿起莫枯修的劍。

「羅密歐，把劍放下，提伯特來了。」班福留說。

羅密歐並未放下劍。「所以你回來看莫枯修死了沒？看我們哭倒在你腳下的樣子？不，不，提伯特！」他大叫。

p. 78–79 提伯特趾高氣昂地走向羅密歐，說：「你這可憐的小傢伙，想和莫枯修一樣找死嗎？」

「我的劍術很強！」羅密歐說著，便舉劍刺提伯特。

提伯特輕易擋住了羅密歐的進擊，羅密歐以迅雷不及掩耳之速繼續攻擊。提伯特想保持冷靜，狀似能輕鬆防衛羅密歐的攻擊。但是沒多久，情勢很明朗，他的對手並不是人，而是復仇天使。

羅密歐使足全力攻擊提伯特，連自己的手或劍都感覺不到了。他猛烈地往前一擊，看到提伯特的眼神從自信變成驚慌，又變成恐懼。

突然間，不聞刀劍聲，也無叫囂。提伯特兇狠的臉變得詳和。就在此時，羅密歐發現他的臉貌似茱麗葉。他看著提伯特倒在地上。

「我們快離開這裡！」班福留大叫：「提伯特死了，親王若發現是你的話，會將你伏法。」

羅密歐丟下劍，劍上沾滿了提伯特的血，茱麗葉兄弟的血。

「喔，我真是個笨蛋！」他說。

「他們來了！」班福留尖叫著說：「羅密歐，快走！」

p. 80–81 茱麗葉站在陽台上，望著夕陽。

「太陽，請離開我們。」她吟唱著：「天色快點變暗，好讓羅密歐快點前來和我相見，讓我們整夜長相依偎。」

奶媽從窗簾外溜到陽台，一臉憂愁。

茱麗葉知道事情不對勁：「發生什麼事了？」

「他死了。」奶媽說。

茱麗葉差點昏倒：「我的羅密歐？我的摯愛？死了？」

「不是，」奶媽回，但情況也相去不遠。「不是，是提伯特，提伯特死了，被羅密歐殺死，而且羅密歐被親王給驅逐出境了。」

「羅密歐真的殺了提伯特嗎？」茱麗葉幾乎不能言語，傷心哭泣。

「這世上沒有正直的男人，」奶媽說：「我希望壞事降臨羅密歐身上。」

茱麗葉爆怒：「不准這麼說！」

「他殺死了您堂哥，您怎能為他辯駁？」

「我該恨自己的丈夫嗎？堂哥也可能殺了羅密歐，但我丈夫還活著。」茱麗葉想止住落淚，「為什麼我止不淚？我該開心的，羅密歐還活著。」

淚水又再度滑落：「驅逐出境！他再也回不了維洛納城，回不到我的身邊了。」

p. 82–83 勞倫斯神父回到房裡，羅密歐站了起來：「神父，怎麼樣？有消息嗎？親王做出判決了嗎？」

勞倫斯神父脫下外套，掛上衣架，說：「很仁慈的判決，」他明白羅密歐並不贊同，「不是處死，是驅逐出境。」

「驅逐出境！」羅密歐大叫：「驅逐出境，比死刑還慘！告訴我是『死刑』吧。」

勞倫斯知道，羅密歐這麼說是因為愛茱麗葉，「親王本可將你處死，但他卻未這麼做，已很仁慈了。」

這時傳來大大敲門聲。

「快躲起來，羅密歐。」勞倫斯神父說。

勞倫斯神父打開門，羅密歐躲藏好。是奶媽。

「午安，神父，羅密歐在這兒嗎？」她說。

「他在這裡，很傷心。」他說，「羅密歐！」

羅密歐走了出來。

「他看來和茱麗葉一樣，」奶媽說：「哭個不停。」

「提到茱麗葉，傷了我的心，奶媽。」羅密歐說。

「您也傷了茱麗葉的心。她想要見到提伯特和你，但卻誰也見不著。」她說。

「我是殺了她堂哥的壞人，」羅密歐說:「我會殺了那壞人，讓茱麗葉開心。」

他抽出了劍，抵著自己的胸膛。

p. 84–85「不要這樣！」勞倫斯神父把羅密歐手上的劍敲掉。「你讓我很錯愕。你誤殺了提伯特，但你要是殺了自己，就等於也殺了茱麗葉。她還活著，你想殺了自己，丟下她嗎？親王才饒了你一命。冷靜點，想想該怎麼做。」

羅密歐癱在椅子上。勞倫斯神父手放羅密歐頭上，「今晚去會見你的摯愛吧，就如同我們計畫好的，去她的房間，安慰她。等見完面，我們再把你送出城。你就先住在曼圖阿，等我們處理好你們兩個家族。如果你的愛夠堅決，愛就會持續下去。」

「好主意，我回去告訴茱麗葉，說你今晚會來。」奶媽說。

卡布萊和巴利斯一起在家。提伯特之死，讓卡布萊明白到許多年輕人根本不聽他的話。提伯特沒聽他的話，所以死了。卡布萊不希望他唯一的女兒，也犯同樣的錯誤。

「夫人，」他命令說，「睡覺前去告訴茱麗葉，跟她說巴利斯愛她。三天後，這個星期四，她就要嫁給巴利斯。」

卡布萊夫人點個頭便離開了。

「這樣你可以嗎？」卡布萊問巴利斯。

「沒問題。我希望我們明天就能結婚。」他回答。

[第五章] 秘密計畫

p.88–89 在茱麗葉樓上的房裡，羅密歐親吻著他的摯愛。

「你為什麼這麼快就要離開？」茱麗葉問。

「我得離開才能活下來，不然就是留下來等死。」

「留下來，我們一起死。」她抱著他說。

他再次親吻她：「我會跟隨妳。」

「我的小姐！」奶媽推開房門輕聲說：「您母親來了。」

「再見了，吾妻，吾愛，」羅密歐說：「再一個吻，我就離開。」

他撥撥她的頭髮，親吻她的額頭。

「我的丈夫，我每天都要聽到你的消息。」茱麗葉說。

「再見了，」他又說了一次：「我會每天寫信給妳！」

「我們何時可以再見面？」

「很快……」

「快點！」奶媽大聲地說。

「我好怕。」茱麗葉說。

「相信我。」羅密歐說。

他吻過她，然後爬下陽台。

「茱麗葉，妳還好嗎？」卡布萊夫人打開門問道。

「不好。」茱麗葉很快地穿好衣服說。

「還在為妳堂哥的死哭泣嗎？」卡布萊夫人問：「我們都很難過。」

p. 90–91 茱麗葉的母親接著告訴她說：「禮拜四早上，妳就要在聖彼得教堂和巴利斯成婚。」

「不，我不要！」茱麗葉不經思索地就喊出口。

卡布萊夫人生氣地說：「妳要違抗我們嗎？」

「我是說，這是不可能的。」茱麗葉說。

房外傳來上樓腳步聲。「妳父親來了，妳自己告訴他。」

卡布萊走進房裡。

「父親，我不能嫁給巴利斯。」茱麗葉說。

「我希望妳可以嫁給他。」卡布萊說。

「我了解，但我就是不能嫁給他。」

「我的期望對妳來說毫無意義嗎？」

「您的期望對我來說很重要，但我就是不能嫁給巴利斯。」

「妳怎可違背我意？」卡布萊大聲說道：「我還是這家的主人嗎？妳禮拜四就和巴利斯成婚。」

「父親，我懇求您！」茱麗葉哭倒在父親腳邊說：「您一向讓我自己作主，求求您，這次也讓我自己決定吧。」

「作主？那我給妳一個選擇。星期四嫁給巴利斯，不然就永遠別再見我。不要再說了！就這麼辦！」他說。

茱麗葉抱著母親哭泣。卡布萊夫人推開她，說道：「妳父親這麼做都只為了妳好，別再多說了。」然後丟下茱麗葉和奶媽離開。

p. 92–93「該怎麼阻止這一切？說話啊！我該怎麼辦？」

奶媽也沒有答案。她只知道，若茱麗葉離開，她就會失去工作，沒法養活自己。

「奶媽？」茱麗葉哀求。

「好吧，我的建議是，她說：「羅密歐被驅逐出境，永不能回來，他是唯一知道妳已結婚的人。當然我知道，勞倫斯神父也知道，但我們都不會透露半句話，妳懂嗎？如果妳嫁給巴利斯，只有羅密歐會對這場婚姻提出異議，但他不可能提出來，因為他永遠都回不了維洛納城。」

茱麗葉愣住了，說道：「妳是認真的嗎？」

她盯著奶媽的眼睛。

「這是唯一的辦法，巴利斯會是個好丈夫的！」她說。

「謝謝妳，奶媽，妳不需要再多說什麼了。」茱麗葉生硬地回答：「去告訴我的父母，我會嫁給巴利斯。」

奶媽看著到茱麗葉走到門邊打開門，感到胃一陣不適。茱麗葉就如她女兒，她來找她求救，而她能做的卻是欺騙。更悲慘的是，茱麗葉明白她在騙她。

「我說我會嫁給他的，奶媽。」茱麗葉雙手交叉著說：「妳可以走了，我明天一早就去找勞倫斯神父，告解我的罪孽。」

p. 94–95 這時，巴利斯正在教堂和勞倫斯神父談話。

「禮拜四太趕了。」神父說。

「這是她父親要求的。」巴利斯回答。

「那茱麗葉怎麼說？」

「她正因堂哥之死而傷心不已，」巴利斯解釋說：「但她父親說她答應嫁給我。」

「我很抱歉，你急於結婚，但你甚至不知茱麗葉心意，我覺得不妥。」勞倫斯神父說。

「勞倫斯神父！」有聲音傳來。

勞倫斯神父往小路看下去，看見茱麗葉正跑過花園。

「喔！有天她也會像這樣呼喊我的名字跑向我。」巴利斯說。

勞倫斯神父假裝沒聽到他的話。「什麼事？」

她看到巴利斯時愣住了。「沒事，神父，我是來告解的。」她說。

「嗨，茱麗葉。」巴利斯打了招呼。

茱麗葉也回了禮，用求助的眼神看著神父。

「巴利斯，請你讓我們獨處一下。」他說。

「當然。茱麗葉，那我們禮拜四見。」他說。

他揮手告別離開。

「喔！茱麗葉，我聽聞妳星期四要嫁給巴利斯。」勞倫斯神父說。

茱麗葉看著他，「沒錯，神父，您一定會阻止這件事。」

勞倫斯神父看著茱麗葉。

「請諒解⋯⋯。」

p. 96–97 「我看明白了。先是奶媽，現在是您。您為我和羅密歐證婚，現在卻不阻止這第二段違法婚姻。」茱麗葉說。

她憤怒離開，卻又突然止步轉身，「你們長輩讓我感到極錯愕。當無事可懼時，你們很勇敢；但一旦麻煩現身，你們就溜之大吉。難道這就是長輩之智嗎？好，我已備好迎接這一切了！」她拿出一把刀來。

「茱麗葉！妳在做什麼？」勞倫斯神父喊。

她用刀子抵住自己的心臟：「既然您幫不上忙，那麼這把刀會解決我們的問題。」

「等等！」勞倫斯神父大叫：「還有個辦法。」

「什麼辦法？」

神父迅速思索著。「這個，」他說著從花園裡拔起一些花，「我會從這些花提煉出一種藥劑，喝下去，人會像死了般睡著。

在妳獨自在房裡時，喝下這藥，妳會感覺到寒冷想睡，甚至脈搏也會停止跳動。之後，等妳家人把妳的屍身抬到家族墓園，我就會去救妳。接下來，我會寫信告知羅密歐此計，他也會前來！請不必驚怕。」

茱麗葉臉上閃過堅決的表情：「把藥給我吧！我不怕。」

勞倫斯神父走進廚房準備藥。

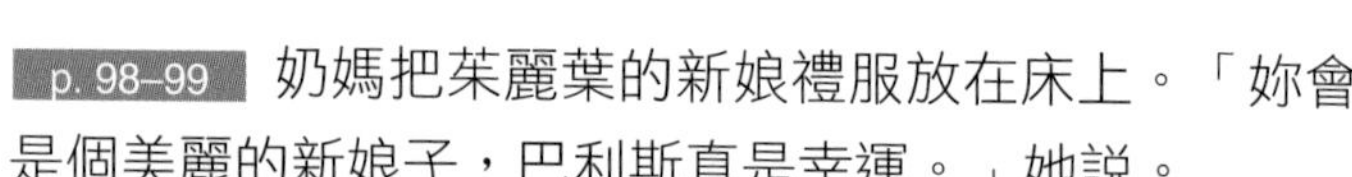

p. 98–99 奶媽把茱麗葉的新娘禮服放在床上。「妳會是個美麗的新娘子，巴利斯真是幸運。」她說。

卡布萊和夫人站在一旁。

茱麗葉看著他們，說：「我很開心能擁有這麼好的父母。」

她鞠躬，嘴角微揚地笑了一下。

「妳真是個完美無瑕的淑女。」卡布萊說。

茱麗葉將禮服移開，坐在床上。

「今晚請容我獨處。我想要禱告。」

「走吧，讓她禱告。女兒，妳讓我很開心。」卡布萊說。

他蹣跚地走出房間。

「今晚需要我陪妳嗎？」奶媽問。

「謝謝妳，」茱麗葉甚至沒瞧她一眼，「沒關係，妳為我做的已經夠多了。」

這些話傷了奶媽的心。

「我願意為您做任何事，您知道的。」奶媽溫柔地說。

「那就讓我一個人待在這裡吧。」茱麗葉說。

奶媽走出房外。

「妳睡一下吧，」卡布萊夫人說，「妳需要的。」言畢便離開。

p. 100–101 茱麗葉靜靜地關上門，拿出勞倫斯神父給的藥，緊緊握著。她閃過一個念頭：如果她在羅密歐到之前就醒了呢？她不會悶死在墓園嗎？更可怕的是，若在那些恐怖的死者圍繞下，她要是瘋了怎麼辦？如果在提伯特的身邊醒來，她會不會瘋掉？如果……？

「夠了，別再『如果』了，」她輕聲說，「這是唯一的解答。」

她把瓶子靠近嘴巴，「羅密歐，這是為你喝的。」便喝下了藥。

她的喉嚨在燃燒，一陣窒息。眼前閃過亮光，身體失去知覺。她感覺到自己倒下，然後就失去知覺了。

天亮前，奶媽醒來，走到茱麗葉房間。她喃喃地說：「我要鼓勵她一下，就這樣，茱麗葉一定會聽我的。」

她打開茱麗葉房門，踮著腳，輕聲地走到床邊。她把手放在她冰冷的額頭上。接著，她的尖叫聲吵醒了全屋子的人。

p. 102–103 永恆的《羅密歐與茱麗葉》

由於莎士比亞描寫主題，普見於世人身上，所以即使到了今天，莎翁的劇作仍然廣受歡迎。劇中人物所經歷的情感與處境，在任何時空、文化皆可見到。這也就是為什麼莎翁的戲劇，能輕易被改編成不同場景，出現在現代電影與舞台劇中。

在莎士比亞的戲劇中，《羅密歐與茱麗葉》大概是最適合改編的作品。世界各地都可見劇場將不同版本的《羅密歐與茱麗葉》搬上舞台，電影導演也會將這齣戲劇翻拍成各具特色的電影。

其中一部最廣為人知的電影，就是 1996 年由李奧納多．迪卡皮歐和克萊兒．丹妮絲所主演的《羅密歐與茱麗葉》。這部電影的背景設定為現代的場景，在電影中，卡布萊與蒙特鳩的年輕人用來打鬥的武器，不是刀劍，是槍枝。

有時電影版本甚至沒提到《羅密歐與茱麗葉》的名字，只是借用當中一些基本的故事情節，1961 年一上映就造成轟動，至今仍受歡迎的《西城故事》，就是一例。

在這部電影中，羅密歐就是湯尼，而茱麗葉就是瑪莉亞。場景是在 60 年代的紐約上西城，一個常發生街頭混混暴力事件、無法無天的社區。湯尼和瑪莉亞分屬於兩個敵對的幫派，但是在這部電影中，瑪莉亞並未喪命。當湯尼遭到敵幫分子槍殺後，瑪莉亞甚至開始計畫讓幫派間能和平相處。

在這些許多不同版本中，莎士比亞這舉世常見的主題，就此繼續流傳著。

[第六章] 戀人悲劇

p. 104–105 當包薩澤打開羅密歐在曼圖阿住處的門時，手發抖著。

羅密歐說：「喔，維洛納城有消息嗎？神父託你送信來嗎？我的父親好嗎？我的茱麗葉好嗎？」

「天使正陪伴著她的靈魂。」包薩澤說。

「她的靈魂永遠都有天使陪伴著，但她其他部分呢？」羅密歐笑著說。

「她的人被送到卡布萊的墓園裡了。」

羅密歐從桌邊站起來：「你說什麼？」

「我……看到她在墓園裡，她……死了。」

「這不可能是真的！」

「我希望那不是真的。」

「去，包薩澤，去牽我的馬來。在城牆邊和我碰頭，我今晚就要動身。」

「請不要去，少爺。您正在盛怒中，這樣是不會有好結果的。」包薩澤說。

羅密歐收拾行李，打包裝進袋子裡。「你錯了，這不是生氣，這是對這種事的合理反應。所以去吧！照我的話去做。」

包薩澤離開了。

「茱麗葉，今晚我就去陪妳共寢。」羅密歐說。

在他遲疑著該怎麼做時，他想起了一件事。曼圖阿有個人專賣奇怪的藥物，他把背包扛在肩上，便走出門。

羅密歐一離開，就有個修道士到了羅密歐住處。

「有人在嗎？」他大叫著：「我送封信要給羅密歐。有人在嗎？是勞倫斯神父寫的信，很重要！有人在嗎？」

無人應門。

p. 106–107 勞倫斯神父躲躲藏藏地走到卡布萊的家族墓園。藉著月亮的位置，他知道現在已經快午夜了，這表示茱麗葉很快就會醒來。他不想去想像茱麗葉在冰冷的墳墓裡醒來時，身邊環繞著骨骸的情景。他快步地走到他指示羅密歐碰面的交叉路口。

那裡沒人。

他等了好久，都沒看到羅密歐的身影。最後，他看到有個人向他走近，但看起來不像是羅密歐。

「還有誰會在這夜深時候來到墓園？」他猜測著。

「是誰？」勞倫斯神父說。

「勞倫斯神父？」有個聲音回應他：「是你嗎？」

「約翰神父？」勞倫斯神父瞇著眼想仔細看清楚是誰。

「是我。」約翰神父說。

「你在這裡做什麼？」勞倫斯神父問。

「羅密歐呢？」

「這就是我來這裡要跟你說的事。」

「你把信交給羅密歐了嗎？」

「我沒機會交給他，我在城門出入之地被耽擱了。」約翰神父説：「等我到曼圖阿時，羅密歐已離開了。」

「喔，不，」勞倫斯神父説，「我相信他這時已聽到茱麗葉的死訊了，而且已經……，親愛的神啊！他做了什麼呢？」

「你看起來很煩憂，親愛的弟兄。」

「去我住所，」勞倫斯神父説：「在那等候，萬一羅密歐在那兒出現，告訴他，茱麗葉還活著。」

約翰神父不明究裡，但他仍依言而行。

p. 108–109 「火把拿著，在這裡等。」巴利斯吩咐隨從。他走到卡布萊家族墓園，隨從在路旁等著。他把花放在墓碑前，「這個，」他告訴自己:「我每晚都會這樣做來證明對茱麗葉的愛。」

他放下花，聽到隨從的口哨聲。是鬼嗎？巴利斯掃過墓園，看到有人靠近。他掩身在大墓碑的後面。

「那不是鬼，」巴利斯想：「是羅密歐！他拿著鐵撬！那殺了提伯特，現在要來破壞墓園了。有我在他就別想得逞！」

羅密歐開始用鐵撬把門打開。

「給我停，你這壞蛋。」巴利斯站出來命令。

「別想阻止我，」羅密歐頭也不抬地説：「別管我！」

門嘎吱一聲地打開，巴利斯用手臂抓住羅密歐。

羅密歐發現巴利斯的手，旋身揮舞鐵撬，正好打中巴利斯的頭。巴利斯倒地而亡，目睹一切的隨從，趕緊跑去通報衛兵。

p. 110–111 羅密歐把巴利斯拖進墳墓裡，在石桌上，他發現了茱麗葉的屍體。

羅密歐跪地，説：「喔，吾愛，吾妻，縱使已逝，妳仍美麗如昔。」

他把茱麗葉的頭髮從臉上往後撥。

「妳是我在世上最想見到的人。」

他親吻她的唇，然後打開一個小瓶子。

「敬我的愛人！」他説罷，便喝下毒藥。

毒藥發作得很快。他又親吻茱麗葉，「有這一吻，我將死去。」

他的身體搖晃，倒地身亡。

「誰在裡面？」勞倫斯神父走進墓園，問道。

他舉起火把，看到巴利斯死在地上，又見羅密歐死在茱麗葉躺著的石桌下方。

「如果我早一個小時到的話，就能救回他們兩人了。」他喃喃自語地説。

茱麗葉呻吟了一聲。「茱麗葉醒了！」

茱麗葉爬起來，看到勞倫斯神父。「神父，我的丈夫何在？」她説。

遠方傳來馬蹄聲。「我聽到有聲音。」勞倫斯神父説：「快離開這裡吧！」

p. 112–113 「羅密歐在哪裡？」茱麗葉問道。

他們聽到聲音越來越近。

「我不能逗留！」勞倫斯神父哽咽説道：「羅密歐躺在地上已死，巴利斯亦已喪命。快點走吧！」

「你走吧！」她跪在一旁，看著羅密歐。

「我的小姐，我得走了！」

「那你走吧，我不走。」茱麗葉説。

勞倫斯神父望著茱麗葉，然後跑出墓園。

「這是什麼？」茱麗葉猜想著：「羅密歐手裡的瓶子？是毒藥。」

她看著瓶子，說：「你全喝光，卻一滴也沒留給我。」她從羅密歐的腰間抽出刀來。

「沒有羅密歐，我也活不下去了。」說完把刀刺進心臟。

她倒在羅密歐身上，親王衝了進來，蒙特鳩隨後進入墓園，卡布萊和夫人也跟進。

「這城市的和平已然破壞了。」親王看著這兩位老人：「我深信這一切皆肇因你們兩家族間的仇恨引起。」

p. 114–115 更多人拿著火把走進墓園裡。

「發生了什麼事？」親王盤問。

一位隊長走進墓園，在親王耳邊低語。

親王點了點頭：「好，把嫌犯帶進來。」

兩名士兵拖著勞倫斯神父進來，丟在地上。

勞倫斯神父辯稱說：「我知自己似乎有罪，但我真的沒有殺害任何人。」

「那這裡到底發生了什麼事？」親王問。

勞倫斯神父一五一十地道來。他說，他已經為羅密歐和茱麗葉證過婚了。

眾人皆驚呼不已。

「當老卡布萊說他要茱麗葉嫁給巴利斯時，她來向我求救。」勞倫斯神父說：「我給了她一瓶讓她喝了可以睡著的藥。若我不這麼做，她就要在我房內自盡。」

「繼續說。」親王說。

「我想告訴羅密歐這件事，但信到得太晚。待我到這裡尋茱麗葉時，羅密歐已先到了。他不知她只是睡著而已，故而自盡。」

他看著巴利斯的遺體：「我猜巴利斯是因為要阻止羅密歐進入墓園，所以才會被殺。我想勸茱麗葉離開，但她就是不願離去。」

p. 116–117 「那你為什麼不留下來陪她？」卡布萊說。

「我很害怕，我是個懦夫。」他哭泣。

「可以了。」親王說，「你是該幫助這些年輕人，但這也不是你的錯。」

親王轉向卡布萊和蒙特鳩兩人。「你們看看兩家長久來的怨恨造成的後果，你們都失去了自己唯一的孩子。」

卡布萊目光從女兒身上抬眼，看到宿敵跪在對面，「蒙特鳩兄弟，請原諒我這一切的仇恨。」他說。

蒙特鳩傾身越過羅密歐與茱麗葉的遺體，環抱著卡布萊：「我會打造一座純金的雕像，來紀念你的女兒。」

「我也會把羅密歐擺在她身邊。」

埃斯卡勒斯親王扶起兩位老人，說道：「我們離開這地方，到別處去談。」

他帶這群悲傷之人走出墓園，「再也沒有比羅密歐與茱麗葉更不幸的故事了。」親王說。

Answers

P. 46	A	❶ (b) ❷ (d) ❸ (a) ❹ (c)
	B	❶ T ❷ F ❸ T ❹ T ❺ F
P. 47	C	❶ (b) ❷ (a)
	D	❹ → ❷ → ❸ → ❶ → ❺
P. 86	A	❶ eager ❷ altar ❸ scolded ❹ pruning ❺ confession
	B	❷ → ❹ → ❺ → ❸ → ❶
P. 87	C	❶ (b) ❷ (a) ❸ (b) ❹ (b)
P. 120	A	❶ tomb ❷ potion ❸ numb ❹ disobey ❺ hobbled
	B	❶ F ❷ F ❸ T ❹ T ❺ F
P. 121	C	❶ (b) ❷ (c)
	D	❷ → ❹ → ❺ → ❶ → ❸

P. 130

A

1. nasty remarks
2. hate, fight, kill
3. reasonable, perfection
4. force peace, fighting
5. banished

B

1. We live by reason, and we die by our passions. (Friar Lawrence)
2. You amaze me, you older people. You are so brave when there is nothing to fear. (Juliet)
3. I would rather die here with you, than live miserably without your love. (Romeo)
4. See what has happened because of your ancient grudge? You've lost your only children. (the prince)

P. 131

C

1. Where did Romeo and Juliet first kiss? (c)
2. Where did Romeo and Juliet decide to get married? (a)

D

1. Juliet drank poison to commit suicide. (F)
2. Romeo wasn't invited to the Capulet's party. (T)
3. Juliet intended to marry Paris. (F)
4. Romeo fell in love twice during the story. (T)
5. Juliet died before Romeo. (F)

羅密歐與茱麗葉【二版】
Romeo and Juliet

作者 _ 威廉・莎士比亞
（William Shakespeare）
改寫 _ Dan C. Harmon
插圖 _ Nika Tchaikovskaya
翻譯 _ 林育珊
編輯 _ 鄭玉瑋
作者 / 故事簡介翻譯 _ 王采翎
校對 _ 楊維芯
封面設計 _ 林書玉
排版 _ 葳豐／林書玉
播音員 _ Kathleen Adriane,
Leo D. Schotz, Tony Eser
製程管理 _ 洪巧玲

發行人 _ 周均亮
出版者 _ 寂天文化事業股份有限公司
電話 _ +886-2-2365-9739
傳真 _ +886-2-2365-9835
網址 _ www.icosmos.com.tw
讀者服務 _ onlineservice@icosmos.com.tw
出版日期 _ 2020年3月 二版一刷（250201）
郵撥帳號 _ 1998620-0 寂天文化事業股份有限公司

Let's Enjoy Masterpieces! *Romeo and Juliet*

國家圖書館出版品預行編目資料

羅密歐與茱麗葉 / William Shakespeare 原著；Dan C. Harmon 改寫 . -- 二版 . -- [臺北市] : 寂天文化，2020.03
面；　公分
ISBN 978-986-318-898-8(25K 平裝附光碟片)

1. 英語 2. 讀本

805.18　　109002022